ISLAND'S END

ALSO BY
Padma Venkatraman

Climbing the Stairs

ISLAND'S END

PADMA VENKATRAMAN

G. P. Putnam's Sons
An Imprint of Penguin Group (USA) Inc.

G. P. PUTNAM'S SONS · A division of Penguin Young Readers Group.
Published by The Penguin Group.
Penguin Group (USA) Inc., 375 Hudson Street, New York, NY 10014, U.S.A.
Penguin Group (Canada), 90 Eglinton Avenue East, Suite 700, Toronto,
Ontario M4P 2Y3, Canada (a division of Pearson Penguin Canada Inc.).
Penguin Books Ltd, 80 Strand, London WC2R 0RL, England.
Penguin Ireland, 25 St. Stephen's Green, Dublin 2, Ireland
(a division of Penguin Books Ltd).
Penguin Group (Australia), 250 Camberwell Road, Camberwell, Victoria 3124, Australia
(a division of Pearson Australia Group Pty Ltd).
Penguin Books India Pvt Ltd, 11 Community Centre, Panchsheel Park,
New Delhi—110 017, India.
Penguin Group (NZ), 67 Apollo Drive, Rosedale, North Shore 0632, New Zealand
(a division of Pearson New Zealand Ltd).
Penguin Books (South Africa) (Pty) Ltd, 24 Sturdee Avenue, Rosebank,
Johannesburg 2196, South Africa.
Penguin Books Ltd, Registered Offices: 80 Strand, London WC2R 0RL, England.

Published simultaneously in Canada. Printed in the United States of America.
Design by Marikka Tamura.
Text set in Mrs Eaves.
Library of Congress Cataloging-in-Publication Data
Venkatraman, Padma.
Island's end / Padma Venkatraman.   p. cm.
Summary: A young girl trains to be the new spiritual leader of her remote
Andaman Island tribe, while facing increasing threats from the modern world.
[1. Apprentices—Fiction. 2. Shamans—Fiction. 3. Indigenous peoples—India—Fiction.
4. Islands—Fiction. 5. Andaman and Nicobar Islands (India)—Fiction. 6. India—Fiction.]
I. Title.   PZ7.V5578Is 2011   [Fic]—dc22   2010036298
ISBN 978-0-399-25099-6
1   3   5   7   9   10   8   6   4   2

To Rainer, with endless love

ACKNOWLEDGMENTS

First and foremost, heartfelt gratitude to my brother Raghu, who provided resources on shamanic healing and strengthened Uido's spiritual journey. Second, my thanks to Thotakar, who showed me long ago that wisdom can exist without formal education.

Several people helped make my time on the Andaman Islands meaningful: John, Paleva, Uncle Pav and the other Karens at the ANET research base; Khan Sahib, Satish, Rom, Harry and others from croc bank who shared their knowledge; Luk, Nikhil and Samir, who remain friends. Macall and Anthony conducted medical research for me; Mark and Michael confirmed my back-of-the-envelope oceanographic calculations; Leland and the Chapins sent journal articles about indigenous people. An early draft of this novel took me to the Highlights Foundation's workshop at Chautauqua, where I found my writing family: Andy, Carolyn, Donna Jo, Eileen, Floyd, Jerry, Jo, Joelle, Kim, Lou, Marileta, Randy, Sneed, Stephen and others whose encouragement I treasure.

In writing this novel, I had the honor to work both with Nancy Paulsen, who guided me to the island's end, and with John Rudolph as my journey began. Thanks also to everyone else at Penguin, including but not limited to Nicole, Tim, Shauna, Susan and the rest of the editorial team at Putnam; Courtney, Eileen, Emily, Jen, Karin, Kim, Kristin, Leslie, Scottie; my agent, Barbara Markowitz; the two Ambujams; and ASTAL, the Boston Authors Club, colleagues, family, friends, librarians, neighbors, readers, teachers and bookstore personnel—too many to name here—for their support.

Hundreds of miles east of India, in the turquoise blue waters of the Bay of Bengal, lie the Andaman Islands. For thousands of years the tropical rain forests that cover this island chain have sheltered tribal people.

When India gained independence from Britain in 1947, laws were created to protect these native islanders and help them preserve their territory and culture. Unfortunately, these laws are not always enforced.

Many surviving tribes now live on reservations run by settlers from the Indian mainland. But even today a few choose to maintain their ancient way of life, despite their close proximity to modern civilization. . . .

I

STRANGER DREAMS

1

My dream begins like all the others I have had about the spirits. I am at the beach on our island. A warm breeze carrying the scent of vanilla flowers caresses my bare skin. Clouds blow like white petals across a blue sky and I hear a beautiful voice singing.

Then the song fades and a woman appears near the shore's edge. She has a round face, soft arms and large thighs. Wondering who she is, I walk toward her. As I come closer, four more limbs grow out of her sides and her body stretches until she becomes gigantic.

An instant later, she floats up above the earth and turns into a dazzling spider. Her eight legs spread out across the sky. Gazing up, I realize she is Biliku-waye, the most powerful of the spirits, who holds the sun and moon and stars in her web each night.

"Go to the beach at once, Uido," she commands. Her voice is beautiful and terrifying.

Suddenly my dream ends and I awake.

Even after I open my eyes, the echo of Biliku-waye's voice is loud inside my head. The sound makes my heart thrash like the wings of a bird trying to fly for the first time. Although I have dreamed of the spirits before, none of them has asked anything of me until now. I sit up and hug my knees, trying to understand why Biliku-waye, the strongest of them all, chose to talk to me—a girl born just fifteen dry seasons ago.

The first finger of sunlight has not yet poked through our thatched roof and my body shivers with awe in the cool darkness. I want to rush to the beach. But that would wake my sleeping family, and I keep my dreams of spirits secret from everyone except my best friend, Danna. I am scared my tribe would find me strange if they knew of my wanderings in the Otherworld. So I wait until I stop trembling and then slowly roll up my reed mat and tiptoe out of our hut. Near the entrance stands the bamboo digging stick that my little brother, Tawai, carved for me. Carrying a stick always makes me feel safer. Trying hard to remain noiseless, I stoop to pick it up, but my grass skirt rustles as I bend.

Outside, a gray mist rises from the ground like a fallen cloud. Our village is quiet, except for the whirr of a bat's wings as it flies into the surrounding jungle.

A whisper breaks the stillness. "Where are you going, Uido?"

I jump like a startled cricket. Tawai stares up at me, his eyes shining with curiosity. Looking at my little brother is like seeing my reflection in a pool, although he is still a child who has lived through just ten dry seasons. His face is as thin and dark as mine, his curls as black and thick.

We are both as skinny as twigs, although Mimi feeds us her share of fatty meat whenever she can.

"Why are you up so early?" I demand.

"You woke me when you picked up your stick," Tawai says.

"You hear well." I pull gently at his earlobe with a teasing hand.

"Where are you going?" Tawai repeats.

"The beach."

"Can I come along?" he asks. For a moment I wonder if I should go alone but I hate refusing him, especially when he sounds so eager.

I nod and Tawai grins, looking as delighted as a monkey biting into a persimmon. He points at the mist. "The skink spirit must have had a big fire last night. Look how much smoke he has blown down from the sky!"

It does not matter that we cannot see very far ahead. The path from our village to the beach where we launch our fishing boats runs east through a short stretch of jungle. My little brother and I have walked it so often that we could find our way there even on a moonless night. Tawai's bow and arrows bounce with every step he takes, and his bone necklace rattles softly. But I tug nervously at my own *chauga-ta* and pray that the ancestors whose bones I wear will help me do whatever Biliku-waye wants.

Soon, the moist undergrowth of the jungle floor gives way to sand that prickles beneath my feet. Tawai almost leaps out of the cover of the trees, but I pull him back.

"Wait." My belly clenches like a fist.

"Why?"

"I—I—something feels different." Biliku-waye's command did not sound like a warning, yet my spirit is uneasy. I sense a change in breeze, as if bad weather is approaching.

"Let go!" Tawai tries to wriggle free.

Still I grip his bony shoulder. The mist is lifting, and staring up the beach to our left, I see nothing but white sand curving into blue water like a crescent moon. To our right, the beach is empty, except for a few crabs scuttling between our canoes and coconut trees. Everything looks the way it always does. As I gaze at the waves twisting along the shore, I feel foolish about my caution. We, the En-ge, are the only people on this island—there is no reason to fear danger.

I am about to let go of Tawai when I hear a voice.

Be watchful.

"Tawai, did you hear that?"

"Hear what?"

I place my finger on his lips to quiet him and listen intently. But it is silent again except for the whisper of the surf.

"Look!" Tawai points to something bobbing on the water far to our right.

His hand reaches for mine. We run along the narrowing stretch of sand to get a better look.

"Maybe evil spirits sent it?" Tawai's voice trembles.

I pull him down onto the sand with me. We hide behind a tall clump of grass.

Lah-ame, our spiritual guide, has told us about people who live on other islands—giants with brown or white skin who travel in boats made of metal. From our cliff top, I have seen the gleam of these boats. And children are often frightened by the drone of the strangers' flying boats, which have wings that never flap as they soar above the jungle, straight and fast—the way this thing is moving toward us now.

"It is a boat," I whisper to Tawai. "Built by strangers from another island."

A faint growl that is not of our world carries across the water as the boat comes closer. I stare at it in wonder. Sometimes pieces of metal wash up on our shores. The elders of our tribe say the strangers make tools from it, and our hunters put it on the tips of their arrowheads because it is harder and sharper than bone. But although metal is heavy as a rock, some magic keeps this metal boat from sinking.

The growl fades as the boat comes to a stop outside our coral reef. I see three men standing on it. Even the shortest man is at least an elbow-length taller than my father, who is the chief hunter and the strongest of the En-ge men. The strangers wear something that is soft enough to puff up in the wind. It covers their bodies, leaving only their arms and legs bare.

Suddenly, a gray glow lights up around the tallest man's head. The skin on my arms grows tight and bumpy with horror. In Lah-ame's stories, a gray aura only surrounds the heads of *lau*: evil white spirits who live in the ocean and bring disease. But as I continue to stare at him, the glow disappears and I wonder if I imagined it.

Together we watch the men lower a small canoe into the water. They climb in and row ashore.

I want to call out to the rest of the tribe and tell them strangers are approaching our island. But the shock of seeing one of Lah-ame's stories come alive makes my voice stick in my throat.

Two of the men stay by their canoe. But the tall one whose head was surrounded by the gray light walks up the sand. A thick mat of hair grows under his long nose, across his cheeks and over his chin. As he comes closer, I see that his legs and even his arms are hairy.

From Lah-ame's stories, I know that a stranger arriving on someone else's shores must shout a request for peace and wait for an answer. But this man is striding up our beach as though it belongs to his people. His rudeness upsets me.

I hear the voice again. *Make him leave.*

Leaping out from behind the clump of grass, I shout, "I am the daughter of the chief hunter of the En-ge!"

The man's jaw drops. I wait for him to ask for peace as he should. Instead, he stares at me.

Holding my digging stick above my head as though it were a spear, I cry, "Go away! Leave our island!"

Following my lead, Tawai jumps up. He pulls an arrow out of his quiver and aims it at the stranger.

The man turns and runs back down to the water. I

shake my stick and chase him, shouting our worst insults, "You long-nose! You sunken-eyed one!"

Tawai is close behind, echoing me. "*Ngig choronga-lanta! Ngig panamaya!*"

Together, the three men shove their canoe into the waves. Their oars slap the water as they row across the reef toward their metal boat and climb back on. We hear a faint growl again. But as their boat moves away from our island, the noise quickly fades. I can hardly believe how fast they go—faster than ten strong men paddling a canoe with all their might.

"We must warn the others," I tell Tawai. But neither he nor I can take our eyes off the strangers' boat. We stand ankle-deep in water, watching until the boat shrinks to the size of a coconut and the blue waves throw it out of sight.

Yet soon enough, our silence is broken by the sound of distant footsteps. Our cries have woken the sleeping tribe.

2

The first person to reach us is my best friend, Danna, his broad fist clenched around his spear. Seeing him arrive, I feel warm with relief.

"Uido! Tawai! Are you all right?" he asks. His usually smiling mouth is a tense line.

"Giant men were here!" Tawai says.

"Who?" Danna looks up and down the sand.

"We chased them away," Tawai boasts.

Danna shakes his head and looks at me. "What happened, Uido?"

"Three strangers came here in a metal boat," I reply. "They were brown as clay and covered with straight black hair." My voice shakes as I remember the frightening gray aura around the tallest man's head.

Our parents come rushing down the beach, followed by others of our tribe. Mimi's long legs carry her slightly ahead of Kara's short ones.

"We are both all right," I say to them.

Slowly, Kara lowers his bow and slings it across his back. "What happened?"

"I frightened three strangers off the beach this morning!" Tawai brags. "They were twice my size but scared of me."

Others of our tribe gather around us. My older brother, Ashu, is at the edge of the crowd, but I can see his neck sticking out far above his shoulders like a heron's.

Tawai tells the story, only he makes it sound as though the boat's faint growl woke *him* up and I followed him to the beach. He confuses everyone enough that no one asks me why we were on the beach so early.

Kara addresses the tribe. "Someone must stay here and warn us if the strangers return," he says. "Our island is too rocky for them to land anywhere else. This is the only place a boat can come ashore."

"I can keep watch," Ashu says.

"I will stay and help," Tawai offers. "I know how to scare them."

"You are a child," Ashu says. "Go back to the village and play with the other little boys."

Mimi glares at Ashu. "Speak kindly to your brother."

Kara tries to make peace. "Tawai, we have not had lizard meat for a while and you are becoming such a good hunter. Will you come with me?"

"Yes!" Tawai says. "We are going to hunt a lizard, a big monitor lizard. My Kara and I, my Kara and I." He runs around Kara, twittering like a parakeet.

"Mimi, shall I go gathering now?" I say. I want to leave the beach quickly, before someone asks me awkward questions. She nods and blows her breath across my face in our gesture of parting.

Danna walks back up the beach with me, away from the rest of the tribe. As soon as we are out of earshot, I burst out, "Last night I had the strangest dream. Biliku-waye appeared and ordered me to go to the beach. That is why I was here so early."

"Biliku-waye?" he says. "Are you certain?"

"Yes. I saw her in both her forms—as a woman and as a spider. Her voice was so powerful it terrified me. And later, on the beach, I heard a voice speaking—as clearly as you are talking to me now—but Tawai could not hear it."

Danna says nothing.

"Do you not believe me?" I ask.

"Of course I do." He squeezes my hand gently.

"There is something else I could not say in front of the others," I continue. "On the beach this morning, I saw an aura shining around the tallest man's head. Like the one that surrounds evil white lau in Lah-ame's stories. For a moment I was scared he was a disease-carrying spirit, but the glow faded very quickly. Is it not strange?"

"I think it is important, not strange," Danna says. "Too important for you to keep your dreams secret any longer. Until now, the spirits only sang to you, and you felt nothing but joy when you were in their world. But last night was different. You must go to Lah-ame at once and tell him you saw Biliku-waye."

Danna's words disturb me. "What if Lah-ame thinks it is bad for me to see the spirits? Maybe he has the power to stop the spirits from ever visiting my dreams again." I shiver despite the growing warmth of the day.

"Even if Lah-ame could use his power to keep you from entering the Otherworld while you sleep, do you really think he would?" Danna gives me a quick hug. "Go now."

He breathes on my face and turns back to the crowd on the beach.

3

I stare at the brown slope of the cliffs lining the northern end of our island where Lah-ame goes to pray every morning during the dry season.

Then I run along the water's edge and plunge into the shadow of the jungle below the cliffs. The earth hardens as the path climbs upward. I splash across a stream that runs downhill. Moments later the jungle is behind me. I run across the dry ground until I reach the tall rock at the tip of our island.

Upon the rock, facing the sun, stands Lah-ame. His black skin gleams like the midnight sky, his hair is as white as a moonlit cloud. The salty breeze carries his deep voice into my ears.

"Biliku-waye, Pulug-ame, spirits of the Otherworld, you decide whether dawn clouds should cover the sky or whether the sun's arrows of light must shoot through the water to wake our reef. You decide if the ocean should rise up tall or send waves that guide our boats carefully through the coral. All-powerful spirits, hear my prayer. Protect us and our island home. Keep our reef sharp. Give strength to the untiring sea so that it batters back all evil creatures."

Still catching my breath, I wait for Lah-ame to sense my presence. This morning the sky looks like the inside of a pearl shell with bands of pink and white shining against the blue. I feel I could almost touch it with my outstretched hand. It seems to hang down low, as close to the earth as in the days of our ancestors, before Biliku-waye's husband, Pulug-ame, shot the arrow that carried the sky out of our reach.

His prayer ended, Lah-ame climbs down from the tall rock and blows his breath across my face in greeting. As always, four feathers from the wings of a sea eagle are tucked into his beaded headband.

"Welcome, Uido," he says. "Are you here to speak with me about your dreams at last?"

His question surprises me so much that I am not sure what to say.

"Yes, Uido." Lah-ame's smile deepens the nest of wrinkles on his face. "I know the spirits visit you."

"But then, why have you never asked me about my dreams before?"

"I have been waiting for you to share your secret with me. Such things must not be hurried." He perches on a nearby stone and motions for me to sit next to him.

I take a deep breath. "Biliku-waye told me to go to the beach this morning. Brown strangers were there. I saw a gray light around one of the stranger's heads and twice I heard a voice speak, though Tawai could not."

"Thank you for trusting me, Uido. And do not worry. I would never tell the spirits to stop speaking to you."

At his words, I am flooded with relief. But a quick shudder runs through me too. How does Lah-ame know everything that is in my mind?

Lah-ame lays his hands on my head. The warmth of his touch comforts me.

Questions roll off my tongue. "How far away do the strangers live? Why did they come here this morning? What magic helps their boats go so fast?"

"The strangers have more things than we can imagine. Huts made of stone. Boats that fly across the ocean and the sky. I was once as young as you are now and just as fascinated by the strangers' magic." Lah-ame pauses. "But we have magic of our own. I found my way into a world that is more beautiful than theirs."

"You mean the Otherworld?"

He nods.

"Can we only travel there in dreams, Lah-ame?"

Lah-ame taps at the side of his head and the feathers in his headband sway. "The Otherworld is inside us and all around us. We may enter it while we are awake as well as when we sleep."

He points at the water. "Look there, Uido. Tell me what you see."

"I see waves chasing each other," I say.

"Look deeper, Uido."

Wondering what Lah-ame wants me to see, I gaze at the bright ocean. It glares back, making my eyes water. But I see nothing unusual.

"Uido, last night, in your dream, you saw with your eyes closed. Try that again."

He rests both his hands on the top of my head again. They grow heavy, weighing down my thoughts until I feel like I am falling asleep on my feet. Slowly, my mind becomes as calm as a pool of water on a still day.

Lah-ame's voice is gentle. "Follow your spirit across the ocean as far as you can."

I am still not sure what he wants me to do, but I imagine my spirit as a circle of light, floating farther and farther away from our island. Suddenly, an image enters my mind of a person standing on a beach. At first the picture is murky but it sharpens as I concentrate. As the vision brightens, my skin tingles and my spirit fills with the same awe as when I dream of the Otherworld.

"I see a beach four times as long as ours!" I say. "I hear the rattling leaves of a coconut palm. A man is standing under the tree and holding his arms out in welcome."

When I finish speaking, the image grows dim. I open my eyes.

He pats my hand. His touch feels as reassuring as Danna's. "I was born on the island you saw, Uido. And the man is my friend."

"Your friend?" I know Lah-ame and the other elders in our tribe were born on another island and that they came here to get away from the strangers. But I do not remember Lah-ame ever saying he had a friend among them. "How could I see him from so far away?"

"The spirits have chosen you to be their messenger because your own spirit has the power to travel deep into the Otherworld. Perhaps you will become the next *oko-jumu*. Would you like to be the tribe's spiritual guide one day? Do you wish to become my apprentice?"

4

Lah-ame's question astonishes me.

"Learn the ways of an oko-jumu?" I whisper. "Me?"

"It is not easy to train as a spiritual guide," Lah-ame continues. "For every ten men who try, nine of them fail."

"But—but"—I stutter, hardly daring to imagine I could someday lead the tribe as Lah-ame now does—"I am a girl."

"Do you not remember the stories I have told about Nimi-waye, Riela-waye, Cormila-waye and Chanelewadi-waye? Those women oko-jumu were also girls once."

"But have *you* known any woman who became a spiritual guide, Lah-ame?" I ask.

"It is rare," Lah-ame admits. "Still, there is no reason why a girl should find it harder to train in the way of the oko-jumu than a boy."

My breath quickens with excitement. "I want to learn everything about the Otherworld."

Lah-ame runs his gnarled fingers over the medicine bag that hangs from his bark belt. "No one can teach you everything. Myself least of all. I only know enough to guide you, if you truly wish to learn."

"I do, Lah-ame."

"This is not a choice to make lightly."

"I feel so alive whenever my spirit dreams of the Other-world. Even seeing Biliku-waye and hearing the voice on the beach filled me with wonder, not just fear. I want to feel that way again."

"Curiosity to explore the Otherworld is good, but not enough. You will need more than curiosity to survive the training. Every apprentice faces tests that threaten their lives. Think it over, Uido. Carefully."

Lah-ame blows his breath on my cheeks, signaling that our talk is at an end.

I linger on the cliff, hoping he will let me stay a little longer. I have so many questions about the Otherworld and training and spirits that no one but Lah-ame can answer.

"You must return to the village now," Lah-ame says.

"But Lah-ame," I say, reluctant to leave his side. "Will you not come with me? Our people will be anxious for your advice about the strangers."

"I will follow you soon enough, Uido."

I sigh and walk carelessly downhill, distracted by the possibilities open before me. A twig snaps underfoot as I enter the jungle, frightening a group of butterflies off a hibiscus flower. As they rise into the air like tiny rain-bows, my thoughts soar up with them. I imagine carrying a pouch full of healing pastes and powders—just like the one that dangles from Lah-ame's belt.

5

I approach the village, my mind overflowing with questions about the oko-jumu life. When I enter the clearing, a drongo bird flies down from the laurel tree behind Lahame's hut. *Tseep–tseep–tseep–tseep*, it whistles, its forked black tail bobbing over my head as if it senses my excitement.

I look for my friend Natalang, with whom I go to gather food from the jungle every morning. The clearing is filled with babies' cries and women's laughter. Mimi kneels outside her youngest sister's hut, combing my little cousin's hair. My aunt sits nearby, suckling her baby. I greet them and ask if they have seen Natalang. They shake their heads.

Natalang's mimi spots me from across the clearing and calls out, "Come and wake my girl, Uido. She is still asleep." Natalang has three older sisters. As the youngest girl in her family, she has very little work.

I go over to her family's hut, opposite ours. Natalang's mimi is rolling wet clay between her fingers and stacking the coils one on top of another to shape a pitcher. "It is good you are Natalang's friend," she says. "If not, that last girl of mine would sleep all day."

I laugh and peer inside their hut. Natalang is sprawled out on her reed mat. Even with her mouth wide open, she is beautiful. Natalang's cheeks are plump as a ripe fruit and every part of her body is round, while my cheekbones are too high and Ashu says I look like a skeleton with skin wrapped around it.

"Wake up." I poke Natalang's soft arm.

She rolls onto her side, knocking over one of the shell plates stacked beside the round wall. Her long eyelashes flutter and she yawns. "It is so early, Uido," she complains, although it is not. "Why are you awake already?"

"Something happened this morning," I tell her.

"Did Danna kiss you at last?" Her eyes widen with excitement.

"Danna is only a friend," I say.

"Then why are you always in such a hurry to finish gathering?" She rolls up her mat and leans it against the curved wall. "We used to be together all the time. But now you want to be with him as much as possible."

Natalang hands me a bark bag for collecting food, picks up her family's wooden water bucket and follows me out of the hut. I know she likes to circle around the clearing, gossiping with the married women and playing with their babies. But I pull at her arm and lead her straight toward the jungle.

Natalang drags her feet, glancing back at the bachelor hut where young men live together when they are *ra-gumul*: the time that comes after they scar themselves with tattoos to prove their manhood but before they marry. It is the only hut without walls and we can see a few boys still pre-paring to hunt or fish, although most have already left.

"So what is it?" Natalang asks when we are inside the jungle.

I want to tell her about Lah-ame's offer to take me on as his apprentice. But now that we are alone, I feel too worried to speak of it directly. Natalang and I have been friends since we were children. Now we are both ra-gumul girls—our blood has come but we are not yet married. Al-though her chatter still lightens my spirit, these days she thinks of boys far more often than I like. Natalang finds it strange that I am not as interested in men or babies, and I do not want her to think me even stranger.

Cautiously, I ask, "Natalang, have you ever wondered how the oko-jumu train?"

She stops walking. "What?"

"Do you ever wonder about Lah-ame's life?"

"Lah-ame's life." She rolls my words slowly in her mouth as if they are berries she is tasting for the first time. "No."

Her simple denial upsets me, because it forces me to see that my interests are drifting even further away from hers. "Why not?" I ask, hoping her answer will somehow make me feel better.

"Probably because he has no wife and no children. I might think of him more often if he had a ra-gumul son."

"But Lah-ame does so much for the tribe, Natalang. He starts our fires, he warns us about bad weather, he heals us and keeps us safe."

"I never said I do not respect him, but even in the dry season when he is in our village nearly every day, his own spirit seems to be in another world."

"Do you ever think about the spirits?" I ask.

"Why would I? Do you?"

"Sometimes." I dig a hole into the ground with my big toe.

"Oh look!" Natalang points by my feet at a tasty *konmo-ta* root. "Help me dig it out."

With my digging stick, I loosen the ground around the fleshy root, and Natalang pulls at it until we work it free. Then she sits back on her haunches and wipes the sweat from her forehead. "So, what was the exciting thing that happened this morning?"

"Strangers came to our island," I say.

"Is that why everyone was shouting? My sisters tried to get me up but I would not open my eyes."

"Only you could sleep through something like that," I tease.

"Did anyone see them up close?" she asks.

"Only Tawai and I. We chased them off the beach. They are much taller than our men, like in Lah-ame's stories."

She giggles. "So are they fatter and handsomer than our men, too? I would like to see these men!"

"Do you think of nothing but men and boys, Natalang?"

"Do you never think of them, Uido?"

I sigh and poke at the ground with my digging stick. The earth feels harder than usual. "Pulug-ame has forgotten to send the rains," I say. "The earth mother is so dry—I am sure Tarai-mimi is ready to quench her thirst."

"You worry too much, Uido," Natalang says. "It is Lah-ame's work to remind Pulug-ame that Tarai-mimi needs a good rain."

One day that might be my work, I think.

Natalang is always happiest in the rainy season, when we move deep into the jungle to the south. There, except for Lah-ame, the whole tribe stays in one communal hut, until the moon has grown into a perfect circle six times and Pulug-ame tires of sending the rain. I enjoy it, but I also miss seeing Lah-ame, who spends most of the rainy season alone, somewhere else.

The rest of the morning we keep busy gathering food. Natalang tells me funny stories, and listening to her cheerful voice, I keep from worrying about the oko-jumu life and the strangers.

A little after midday, we make our way to the pool near the village to fill Natalang's bucket. She dips her finger into the water.

"It is cold!" she shrieks, but she jumps in, startling a nearby frog that leaps away croaking *rrrrgup, rrrrgup*. I wade in after her.

"A crocodile!" she whispers, pointing at something behind me.

I whirl around. "What? Where?"

"You believed me." She laughs. "I never thought you would."

I shake my head at my own foolishness. We all know crocodiles live far away in the swamp that we avoid. I snatch her bucket, half fill it with water and empty it over her shoulder. She squeals and splashes me back, spraying water into my face.

For a while, we laugh and play like when we were little children. But as we clamber up the bank again, a drum-beat booms through the jungle from the direction of the village: *Come, En-ge, come.*

Lah-ame uses this signal to gather the tribe together when he has something important to say.

6

We return to the village. Natalang sways gracefully, balancing the bucket of water on her head, while our bag full of roots bounces against my hip. We part ways as I run into the clearing a few steps ahead of her, eager to hear what Lah-ame has to say.

Mimi takes our heavy bag of food from me. A few moments later, I see Kara emerge from the jungle with a small group of men. A freshly killed monitor lizard dangles from his shoulder. The *petie-ta* is nearly as long as Tawai, who comes running toward me waving his spear and looking as proud as if he hunted the lizard all on his own.

I watch other families knotting together: men bringing fish or animals for the tribe, girls with gathering baskets or bags, married women carrying babies on their hips or holding children by the hand, elders looking as wide-eyed and curious as the children. Only the ra-gumul boys from the bachelor hut sit in a group by themselves rather than with their families.

Lah-ame faces us, standing in front of his hut. The laurel tree behind it casts a long shadow on the ground before him. His palms fly across the boar-skin mouth of his waist-high drum.

I hear the drumbeat soften. "Is anyone missing?" Lah-ame asks.

The married men in each family answer this question in turn. Satisfied that all forty families are present, Lah-ame says, "You must have questions about the strangers who came to our island this morning. As some of you know, I have a friend among them. But most strangers are not to be trusted. So be wary of them."

The elders nod to show they agree with Lah-ame. But the children look confused and a few men shout questions: "Why did they come?" "When will they come again?"

"One of us must keep watch for the strangers during the day to find out why they want to come ashore," Lah-ame answers. "We need not keep watch at night. I know they will not come after dark."

"Why are they as hairy as rats?" Tawai asks.

A ripple of laughter spreads through the tribe.

Lah-ame holds up his hand for silence. "I will answer your questions with a story. But first, we will have our evening meal. I see our chief hunter has brought us a fat lizard."

"Thanks to the help of many," Kara says. He places the dead lizard on the ground at the center of the clearing. Kara and his group of hunters dance out the story of the hunt to honor the animal's spirit. Other groups of men follow.

Meanwhile, Natalang, I and the other ra-gumul girls

empty the food we gathered onto a leaf mat spread on the ground. Soon it is piled high with fruit, nuts, roots, leaves, coconuts and ripe berries. Mimi, as wife of the chief hunter, leads the married women as they cut and skin the animals, laughing and talking.

When they are done, Lah-ame starts a fire. Usually, I find it fascinating to watch. But this evening I am impatient to hear Lah-ame's story about the strangers and I hardly listen to him lead us in prayer to thank the spirits for the fire and the food.

The women roast the meat and fish and make a stew from crabs and turtles. Natalang chatters with them while the stew bubbles and fills the air with cooking smells. I am quieter than ever, waiting for the meal to be over.

Finally, the food is ready—but it seems to take forever for everyone to finish eating. After all the food is eaten, we wipe our hands with clay and sit cross-legged around the fire, picking our teeth clean with fish bones.

At last, Lah-ame rises to begin the story. His voice is a singsong chant, like the wind that rolls over the ocean.

"Tonight is the time for an old tale that you have heard before. But listen well because it carries the knowledge we need to choose our path in the future."

It is silent except for the crackle of the fire in the clearing and the rustle of leaves in the dark jungle beyond.

"In the days of our ancestors, there were as many tribes living on the islands as there are fingers in eight hands. For our ancestors, life was easy, with food and space enough for all.

"We, the En-ge people, shared one great island with many other tribes. Sometimes we fought, but mostly we treated one another with respect. Once in a while we traded things, or danced together. More rarely still, the men of one tribe would marry the women of another and move away. Hardly ever did the En-ge use their weapons on people. We made arrows and spears to fish and hunt—not weapons to kill other men.

"Then one day pale strangers came, their skin white as lau. They trapped us inside nets as though we were fish and dragged us into boats larger than our huts. Our men tried to fight but the pale strangers killed many of them with sticks that shot bursts of fire. The captured En-ge were never seen again.

"Many hunters left our island to seek out the strangers and fight them. But few of these brave ones returned. Those who did brought tales of the strength and cruelty of the pale people, who they said were far greater in number than any of us could imagine.

"Still, there were two things for which our ancestors were grateful. The pale strangers never came during the rainy season, when Pulug-ame sent howling winds and jagged waves. And the strangers did not want to live on our islands.

"Not until the days of my grandfather's grandfather did a group of pale strangers come to stay. But when they did, they cut down trees and built stone huts in their place. They did not always eat the birds and animals they killed. And they brought with them a stinking water that burned the throat and drowned the spirit. Men who drank of this water often turned against one another.

"Worst of all, the pale strangers brought disease. They carried lau that did not cause their own people any harm, but killed us. These lau spirits leaped out of their bodies and into ours so fast that every oko-jumu was helpless against them. For the ways of the oko-jumu are slow and lau are quick to spread death.

"Many tribes died out. One by one.

"By the time of my birth the pale strangers had left the islands. But now the islands were overrun with strangers who had brown skin. These brown-skinned ones did not capture us in nets or bring us evil water. But they, too, showed no respect for Biliku-waye and Pulug-ame. And they, too, brought disease.

"The clear waters of our streams became muddy as these strangers cut down the trees, and our jungle began to shrink like a withering fruit.

"As a ra-gumul boy, I was both scared and fascinated by the strangers' powerful magic. So I traveled to their village in secret. There, I saw how different their lives are from ours.

"To us, the tribe is one large family. But in their greed to hoard magical things, the strangers rarely share all they have with one another. So their spirits are empty. They try to fill their loneliness with noise and have forgotten the beauty of silence.

"By shutting out the spirits of earth and water and air and light and living far apart from the spirits of trees and animals, the strangers crush their own spirits. And thus they lack something the En-ge have. The strangers rip out of themselves the joy that we carry deep inside, even those among us who are not oko-jumu. When our feet stamp the earth and our voices rise in joy, when our laughter shakes our bodies from toe to belly to shoulder, its echoes fill the Otherworld.

"I decided that it was best for the En-ge to keep their own spirits happy and safe by moving away from the brown strangers. I wanted to find another island to live on—one that we did not have to share with them.

"So I called on the sea eagle, who is my spirit animal, for help. Kolo-ame took me far on his broad back. On his wings I flew and through his eyes I saw this green pearl of an island waiting for us.

"I spoke of this island to the oko-jumu who was training me. He allowed me to address the tribe. But he and most of the others chose to stay where they had been born.

"Our tribe was torn apart like a leaf in a storm. My oko-jumu remained on the island with the many hundreds who refused to leave. And I led the few who believed in me to this island where we now live.

"Around our island the spirits drew a circle of sharp coral to guard our shores like a wall of spears. Once we arrived, they raised stormy waves to protect us. Here we have celebrated many happy seasons of dry and rainy weather. Only a few of us remain who remember that day long ago when we split away from the others in our tribe and journeyed to this island. Yet with the strangers' arrival, the question will soon arise again about where and how we shall live.

"Today, strangers set foot on our island. Their ways are not our ways. Their world has no place for us. And you must decide if you wish to make a place for them in ours.

"This is a story I have told before, but now I give it as a gift to each of you. Remember it well. May it serve to guide your actions long into the future."

In the firelight, all our shadows seem to bind together for a moment into a thick rope. Before anyone speaks to him, Lah-ame disappears into the jungle like dark smoke in the night sky.

7

Lah-ame's story leaves me wondering what choices I will face if I become an oko-jumu. And whether I will ever have the courage to challenge the rest of the tribe as he did.

Later that night, I feel a strange pull, as though someone were tugging at a rope tied around my belly.

I follow the spirit-pull away from the village, through the jungle trees and to the beach. Standing alone on the sand, I gaze at the spot where the strangers arrived.

The ocean looks inviting. I wade into the shallows. The water slurps around my thighs, tugging me deeper in. But at the same time a breeze stirs and pushes me gently back toward the shore. It is as though the sea is asking me to explore all that lies beyond our island, while the jungle wants me to remain safe within it.

I go a little farther into the water, until it encircles my waist. But the current feels stronger than usual, so I climb out of the surf and walk up the beach with sand sticking to my wet feet.

I hear something slither behind my heels and look back. Sea snakes are crawling out of the water, the black and white bands on their long bodies shining in the moonlight. They rarely bite, yet I know they are more poisonous by far than any land snake. One drop of their venom is enough to kill a strong man. And they are most dangerous when they come ashore to lay eggs.

In a few moments they are wriggling all around me. Trapped halfway between the ocean's edge and the jungle, I stand, waiting for the snakes to pass. Sweat bursts like dew on my palms.

I watch the snakes' backs, curving in endless lines of black and white. They are as beautiful as they are terrifying, like Biliku-waye in the Otherworld. Wave after wave of them goes by, making me dizzy. My body sways like a coconut tree in a storm.

Keep your balance.

I gaze at the sand, which is alive with movement. Balance. I put one foot forward. Then the next.

Already you are a little closer to safety.

I take another step and another. My toes find empty patches of ground between the snakes' wriggling bodies. Dancing on tiptoe, I reach the jungle. The shadows of trees reach out and embrace me. There are leaves underfoot again.

Moments later, I am inside the dark circle of our village. Then at last the round walls of our home protect me. I lie on my mat, gazing at the dots of starlight that pierce through our thatched roof.

Finally, I drift into sleep.

8

I awake at dawn, unsure whether snakes really crept up the sand last night or if it was another vision. I hurry to the beach to look for the telltale signs of snake paths. But I see only the gentle marks left by the receding waves.

Later, as Natalang and I head toward the jungle to gather food, confused thoughts buzz in my head louder than the cicadas in the trees. She chatters away as usual, but I hardly listen.

My toe bumps against a gnarled root jutting out of the ground and I almost fall. Natalang catches hold of my arm to steady me.

"You are stumbling over every clump of leaves today," she says. "Is something wrong?"

"It is the story Lah-ame told us last night. It was not new but I felt like I never truly listened before."

"Not Lah-ame again!" Natalang pretends to yawn. Then she mimics Lah-ame's singsong chant. "Today is the time for a new tale, a story we have all been waiting for. One day a boy named Danna, whose teeth were as white as coral in the moonlight . . ."

I pluck a handful of berries off a nearby bush and crush

them on top of her head. She giggles, wiping off the juice that drips down her nose.

"Those berries are overripe." Natalang waves her fore-finger at me. "Now be quiet, Uido, and listen. You need to learn more about boys."

I shake my head and try to mimic her voice. "Not boys again!"

She ignores me and fills me in on the gossip about the new ra-gumul boys who have entered the bachelor hut and which girls she thinks they like.

She goes on and on, and I stop listening.

We return to the village at dusk, my spirit as heavy as my full basket. I see Danna approaching from the opposite direction, waving a net bag full of fish. "Uido! Natalang!" he calls out.

Natalang runs over and blows her breath across his face in greeting. "What a large catch! Who helped you get so many?"

"All thanks to Biliku-waye and Pulug-ame," Danna says, but his cheeks redden with pleasure at Natalang's compliment. "What have you two brought back for us?" He slips Natalang's bag off her plump shoulder. "Now, that is heavy."

"Not as heavy as Uido's bag. Do you want to see what she has?" Natalang gives Danna a knowing smile.

My face grows warm with embarrassment. But Danna replies without any shyness in his voice, "I do want to speak to her alone."

"You have secrets to tell Uido?" Natalang pushes her

lips into an overdone pout. For a moment I am afraid she is truly annoyed to be left out. But she bursts out laughing.

"Go on, both of you." She makes kissing noises as Danna and I walk away into the evening shadows that darken the jungle.

We slip behind the stout black trunk of a *moro-ta* tree. I rest my back against its rough bark.

"Did you talk with Lah-ame?" Danna asks.

"He asked if I wanted to learn how to be an oko-jumu!"

Danna's broad grin widens. "Uido, our spiritual guide. I always knew you were special."

"You would not stop being my friend if I said yes?"

"Why would you think that?" His smile disappears and he sounds hurt.

"When I tried to talk about the Otherworld with Nata-lang, she would not listen. And she thinks it is strange that I care about Lah-ame's stories."

"I am not Natalang."

"But Danna, it worries me that Lah-ame has no family. Or close friends, even. All the other men go hunting in groups—but he leaves early every morning to pray on the cliffs. In the evenings, though he is with us, he starts the fire by himself and hardly speaks to the other elders while he eats."

Danna grasps my hand. "Nothing will stop me from being your best friend. And yes, Lah-ame is often alone, but that does not mean every oko-jumu's life is similar to his. He has told us stories about other spiritual guides—

men, and even women, who married and had children. Surely you can be more like them."

I nod, pleased that Danna remembers the stories of women who became oko-jumu.

He looks deep into my eyes. "There is just one important question, Uido. Do you want to become Lah-ame's apprentice?"

"I do, Danna, more than anything else. In the Otherworld my spirit feels as though it touches something endless. Like I am one tiny bead on a giant necklace, but also the necklace itself." I pause. "But Lah-ame spoke about how painful and hard the training and the tests will be. I am scared. What if I fail?"

"Would you feel better if you never tried?"

A sudden rustle in the bushes near us startles me. Danna pulls an arrow out of his quiver and whirls around, looking for the source of the noise.

"Ashu!" My shock turns to irritation when I realize my brother was hiding in the darkness.

"Why are you stalking us like a cat?" Danna's voice is thick with annoyance. "I almost shot at you!"

Ashu's lips curl derisively. "You are too slow to shoot me."

Danna grits his teeth, as though he is trying to bite back angry words.

Ashu turns on me. "If you have special powers, why did you not see me hiding all this while?"

"Not even Lah-ame knows everything, Ashu," Danna says.

"He certainly knows nothing about my sister. I cannot believe Lah-ame thinks she could become oko-jumu. None of the spirits talk to her."

"They do," I say, struggling to remain as calm as Danna.

"Prove it to me, then," Ashu challenges. "Make a prediction. Surely you can look into the future and tell us when the strangers will come next?"

"No, Uido." Danna grabs my arm as if to try and hold me back. "You do not need to prove anything to Ashu."

I jerk my arm free although I know Danna is right. I am tired of controlling my anger while Ashu insults me. If there is any way to see into the future using the Otherworld, I feel determined to find it.

With my eyes closed, I try to imagine my spirit as a circle of light—just as when Lah-ame guided me to see far across the ocean through the Otherworld. But the spirits seem unwilling to let me in this time. However hard I concentrate, the circle of light keeps disappearing. And when I search for an image in my mind, all I see is a dark wall.

Feeling too angry at Ashu to give up, I imagine myself pounding at the wall with my fists, repeatedly shouting Ashu's question about the strangers. I refuse to stop until I force an answer out of the Otherworld. At last, a whisper comes through the darkness in my mind, a single word.

Tomorrow.

"Tomorrow." The moment I say the word aloud, I regret it.

"We shall find out," Ashu says.

I see a flicker of resentment in his eyes before he turns to leave. He strides away to the village ahead of us. We follow, taking care to keep our distance from Ashu.

"Please," I whisper to Danna. "Do not tell anyone what I said about the strangers coming tomorrow."

"Why not?"

"The spirits did not want to let me into the Otherworld—I forced myself in for the wrong reasons. Maybe they felt upset and lied to me."

"Will you at least let Lah-ame know what happened?"

"What if he gets angry that I tried to prove myself to Ashu? Let us just wait and see what happens. Ashu will surely tell no one because he would not want anyone else to know Lah-ame offered to teach me."

Danna reluctantly agrees to keep our secret.

All evening I cannot help wondering if my behavior angered the spirits. That night, I squirm restlessly on my mat, wishing I had listened to Danna and ignored my older brother's taunts.

9

The next day, I wake much later than usual, with no memory of any dream. My mind is like a beach without footprints and I worry that the spirits kept me out of the Otherworld because they are angry about yesterday.

Mimi bends over me and runs her hand over my forehead. "Are you unwell, Uido?"

"No." I sit up at once.

"It is not like you to sleep so late."

"Please do not worry, Mimi. I am not hurting at all. I will go shellfish collecting. Now."

At the sound of my voice, Tawai bounds into the hut. "Can I come with you, Uido? I want to fish."

Ashu's form darkens the entrance. He sticks his head in only for a moment to say, "I will go to the beach as well."

I hurry out into the sunshine and run across the clearing to invite Natalang along too. It is late enough that she is awake. She brings a new basket she has woven out of bamboo—strong enough to hold any clams or mussels we gather at the shore.

As we walk down to the beach, Ashu surprises me by being unusually polite to Natalang.

"This is a beautiful basket," he says to her, running his long fingers across it. "Very well made."

For a moment I think he is being sarcastic, but Natalang blushes at his compliment. She walks between me and Ashu and although she links arms with me, she speaks only to him. Tawai skips along beside us.

The short path to the beach feels as long as a day's walk. All the while, I wonder whether my prediction of the strangers' arrival will come true and how Ashu will treat me if it does not.

We are nearly at the beach when my nose catches a faintly bitter smell—like smoke though not the scent of burning wood. I run to the edge of the jungle and see the strangers' boat jutting above the waves like a gigantic shark fin.

"Look," I cry. "I was right."

I dash toward the tall grass where Tawai and I took cover the first time we saw the strangers. Danna is already crouched there, his eyes on the strangers.

Danna looks relieved to see me. "I took the watch today," he says as we all huddle behind the grassy clump. "I knew you would be right, Uido."

"Do not call the tribe yet, Danna," I say. I am curious to see why the strangers have come back and I do not want them to be frightened into leaving too soon.

The strangers' boat stops just beyond the edge of our

reef and the same three men lower their canoe over the side. We watch them climb in and row carefully past the coral, toward the beach.

I feel Tawai move closer to me, his breath fearful and excited on my shoulder.

"Should I not alert the village now, Uido?" Danna fidgets.

"Why are you asking her?" Ashu hisses. "Since when did the tribe start taking orders from girls?"

The men row closer. The tall man seems to be the leader. He jumps into the surf before the others and works hard to pull their canoe up the beach while the other two push it out of reach of the waves.

"Nice fat bodies," Natalang whispers to me. "But too much hair on the face."

The men unload their canoe, piling coconuts and bananas on the ground.

"Why do they bring us gifts after we chased them away?" I say uneasily. "They are not our friends."

"Look at that yellow hill of bananas!" Natalang rolls the tip of her tongue across her lips. "I wonder how they taste."

Ashu grins at her. "Come, Natalang," he says. "I am not afraid of these strangers."

"No," I tell them. "Wait. We should call the rest of the tribe here to decide what to do."

"I am your older brother and the son of the chief hunter," Ashu says. "I am not taking orders from you." He stands up and holds his hand out to Natalang.

Natalang lets Ashu pull her to her feet. "You are so brave, Ashu," she says.

I want to say, "Natalang, you are *my* friend. You know Ashu is often mean to me!" But choking with disbelief, I watch Natalang hold hands with Ashu and run toward the mound of bananas, her breasts bouncing.

"Wait for me," Tawai says. I lunge out to stop Tawai but he races away over the white sand, the pink soles of his feet flying. As I leap up and chase after my little brother, I hear Danna call out, "*Olaye, olaye, odo-lay, odo-lay!* Come, everyone! The strangers are here again!"

Two of the men turn back and start running toward their canoe, away from Ashu and Natalang, who are headed toward the bananas. But the leader seems surprisingly less afraid of us today, and that only deepens my unease. He watches Tawai and me approach while his friends push the canoe into the water.

Tawai runs up to him, ignoring my anxious cries.

The man smiles at Tawai but his small eyes shift from side to side. "Ragavan," he says to Tawai, patting his chest. "Ragavan."

"Tawai," my brother says, patting his own chest. He reaches up and grabs at something box-shaped that hangs from a black strap around the man's neck. The strap does not look like it is made from vine or the skin of any animal we have on our island. And the box itself is much smaller than our boxes—too small to store much of anything.

Ragavan holds the box in front of his eyes. It hisses and

then makes a quick, sharp noise. He bends down and shows the box to Tawai. Curiosity tugs me forward like a strong current, and half unwillingly I step closer to see what the box does.

"There is a painting of me inside!" Tawai shrieks. "This is a magical box!" Tawai jumps up and tries to snatch the box. Ragavan holds it out of our reach but keeps the box steady so I can have a good look. Inside it, I see a small image of Tawai and everything around him.

How can the box make such a perfect shrunken picture? Has it caught a piece of Tawai's spirit?

Facing me, Ragavan raises the box in front of his eyes again.

"No!" I say firmly. I hide my face with my hands to make it very clear I want no painting of me.

But Ragavan ignores my wish. I hear the box hiss and click again.

Once again I see a gray aura flicker around Ragavan's head for a moment and then disappear. Everything about Ragavan seems wrong. All the anger I feel—at Ragavan, at Ashu and at Natalang—pours out of me.

"Ragavan, go!" I point at his boat. "Leave. Now."

Ragavan seems to understand my outburst. He turns and runs to join the other two strangers, who are waiting for him in the canoe.

Behind me, I hear footsteps coming, loud and fast. Kara and his hunters race down the beach in time to watch Ragavan and his friends pull away.

"Are you all right?" Kara puts his arm around me.

I nod weakly as the anger that strengthened me moments ago drains away. I hear the growl of the metal boat moving away from our island. Resting against Kara's stocky body, I watch our people come swarming across the beach like ants on an anthill.

A few elders question Danna about what happened. They seem worried, but the ra-gumul boys talking to Ashu look excited. So do the women, children and ra-gumul girls crowding around the strangers' gifts of fruit. I hear a woman squeal, "This mound of coconuts is nearly as tall as my baby!"

I walk over. Natalang rushes up and puts her arm around my shoulders. But she does not seem to realize I feel hurt that she abandoned me and ran away with Ashu.

"Uido, why are you so worried about these strangers?" she asks. "Lah ame said he had a friend among them. And look how much food they brought. If these strangers came every day, we would never need to go gathering!"

Natalang's mimi overhears her and laughs. "It is good they do not, or you would do nothing but sleep."

I decide not to speak about the way Natalang acted with my brother. After all, she quickly shifts her attentions from one boy to another. Perhaps the less I say, the sooner she will forget about Ashu.

I let Natalang pull me toward a pile of fruit. She peels a banana and bites into it. "Very sweet," she says, her mouth full.

I take a tentative bite out of one that she waves under my nose. It smells overripe and feels soft, not like the green, firm bananas we usually eat. But looking at the happy faces around me and listening to the chatter of women's voices, I realize none of them share my dislike of the strangers' gifts—not even Mimi.

Although I am surrounded by the women of my tribe, I feel lonely. I seem to be one of the few who remembers Lah-ame's story and his warning to be careful of the strangers. But seeing the anxiety in the faces of the elders, I realize I need to do more than chase Ragavan off the beach each time he arrives. With the help of Lah-ame and the spirits of the Otherworld, I must learn how to protect my island from being overrun by the strangers, the way the beach was overrun by venomous snakes.

10

I slip away from the rest of the tribe and walk along the curved beach toward the cliffs. As I run up the jungle slope, a nervous excitement rises inside me.

I find Lah-ame praying on the tall rock just as he was the morning after my dream of Biliku-waye.

He climbs down, holds his arms out to me in welcome and says, "Uido, are you here to tell me your decision?"

"Yes. Today on the beach, I sensed that the strangers' ways threaten our own. I want to become your apprentice so I can learn how to protect our tribe and keep our people's faith in our old ways."

"Are you certain, Uido? You are willing to risk losing your mind or your life?"

"Yes," I reply. "Though I am a little scared."

Lah-ame's bird-bright eyes sparkle. "A little fear is good."

"Lah-ame, I did something wrong," I blurt out. "I tried to force the spirits into talking to me just to show Ashu I could enter the Otherworld."

"It is not the first time you have been foolish, Uido," Lah-ame says. "And it will not be the last. But you are right to regret what you did. Until you go further in your training, it will be best if you do not send your spirit into the Otherworld while you are awake—unless I am at your side, guiding you."

"So you are not angry? You will still teach me?"

"Everything I know," he says.

"Will we begin my training soon, Lah-ame?" I do not want to wait another day.

Lah-ame smiles and lays a gnarled finger on my lips as if he were trying to quiet a baby. "Tomorrow morning I will gather the En-ge together and say why I have chosen you as my apprentice. It is best if everyone hears this from me at the same time. After that, they will move south for the rainy season. And you and I will move away to another part of the jungle, where we will walk the spirit paths together."

I slap my thighs with my palms to show my joy.

Lah-ame scoops me onto his back as though I were as little as Tawai. We laugh, and his laughter seems to roll out from the pit of his stomach and rise up beyond the cliff top. As he carries me down toward the village, I feel sure that all the spirits of the Otherworld can hear us.

11

Lah-ame drops me off his back under the laurel tree behind his hut and strides into the clearing. I follow him into the village, almost dancing.

Everyone seems to be chattering about the strangers. But the talking stops when Lah-ame beats his drum.

"The rainy season approaches," Lah-ame tells us. "The wind spirit blows from a different direction, the ocean's waves leap high and the *guru-ta* caterpillars are turning into butterflies. It is time for the tribe to leave the spirits of the plants and animals that live around our village to refresh themselves, while we move south for the rainy season."

"What about the strangers?" one of the ra-gumul boys asks. "What if they come ashore while we are in the south?"

Lah-ame replies, "Although their boats are stronger than ours, the strangers would never dare to fight past the crashing waves of the rainy season. The water spirit's power and Pulug-ame's storms will make it impossible for them to land on our shores."

The elders nod in agreement, which seems to satisfy the village.

"We may eat the food the strangers brought, may we not, Lah-ame?" a woman asks.

"I dislike the strangers' gifts but it is wrong to waste food." Lah-ame hesitates for a moment. "Since they brought so much food, no one need go hunting or gathering today. Instead, you may spend the rest of the day preparing for the journey south. Tomorrow morning, you will leave."

Lah-ame puts away his drum and the rest of us start preparing for the move.

Natalang's mimi and some of the other married women kneel beside the trunk of a palm tree they have cut in half. They pull out the white fiber inside, while Natalang and some of the other ra-gumul girls grind the fiber into a powder. I picture the tribe sucking handfuls of the sweet powder while they walk tomorrow so that no one gets too tired. It saddens me that for the first time since I was born I will not be with them.

Not far away, Mimi and Kara are busy covering each other's bodies with the mixture of clay and turtle fat that we use to keep mosquitoes away in the rainy season. Kara's eyes glisten like the fresh paint on Mimi's back when he looks at her, as though they were married only yesterday. I want to rush up and hold them close, bury my head in Mimi's long arms.

Instead, afraid that tears might spill down my cheeks if I imagine tomorrow's parting, I head back to our hut. I pass by Tawai and his friends, who are taking turns clinging to a vine that hangs down from a tree behind the bachelor hut.

Tawai stops swinging and jumps to the ground. "Uido! What were you doing with Lah-ame this morning? I saw him carrying you on his back."

I avoid answering his question. "Are you and your friends going to help prepare for tomorrow's move or are you planning to swing on vines all day?"

"Maybe I could help Ashu make some hunting tools!" Tawai says. I see our older brother outside our hut, sticking a feather onto his arrow shaft with beeswax glue. Running up to him, Tawai asks, "Will you teach me to make a spear?"

"No," Ashu says. "You are too young."

Tawai's face crumples like a leaf crushed underfoot. But before I can do anything to make him feel better, Danna walks over and offers to show Tawai how to carve a bamboo carrying frame.

My secret almost bursts out of me when I see Danna. I whisper, "I spoke to Lah-ame this morning."

"You have decided?" he asks softly.

I try to keep my voice steady as I reply, "We must not speak of it yet."

A wide smile spreads across Danna's face. He puts his arm across his chest, as though to clasp my secret to himself.

When at last the day is over, I stretch out on my reed mat and Tawai huddles close to me, yawning. His chauga-ta pokes into my shoulder, but I do not complain. I finger the bones of our ancestors that are strung around my own neck and pray to them to help me survive the oko-jumu training and return safely to my family.

That night, for as long as I can I keep awake, taking in the warmth of Tawai's and Mimi's bodies on either side of me, the sound of Kara's snore and the smell of the fresh paint on their skin. Lying in the darkness, I wonder what the training will be like and how long I must stay away. Tomorrow I will have to sleep all alone—something I have never, ever done. Despite my eagerness to learn, it will be hard to live apart from my family and Danna and Nata-lang and the rest of the tribe.

The next morning, as soon as Lah-ame beats his drum, my heart skips with excitement again.

We gather in a loose circle, the way we always do before the journey south. Mimi hands Kara a cone woven out of palm fronds and he fills it with embers from last night's fire. Each of his hunters carries a similar torch, with embers that they must keep alive to kindle fires all rainy season while Lah-ame is away.

Holding the torches high above their heads, Kara and his hunters move up front, where they will lead the men forward on the four-day walk. I stay together with the women, children and elders who will follow behind. Mimi carries a basket full of Kara's tools and hunting weapons. I feel guilty knowing I will not be able to help her with the load on the long walk ahead.

Once we are all assembled, Lah-ame says what I am

waiting for. "I have something very important to tell you before the tribe moves south. The spirits have chosen the one they wish to be their next messenger."

I hear voices crackling with excitement as my people try to guess who Lah-ame's apprentice will be. He continues, "For a while we hid from the strangers, but now that they have found us again, they may not leave us to ourselves. The strangers will likely keep returning to our island, bringing with them new ways and new things. We must find a leader to hold this newness together with our old ways. And in times of change such as this, a woman must lead the tribe."

"A woman?" Cries of surprise burst from the tribe. I turn to see Natalang next to me. She whispers, "Imagine that, Uido!" Only the elders nod as if they expected Lah-ame to say this.

A girl's voice rises above the others. "Have there been other women oko-jumu?"

"Those of you who listen well to my stories," Lah-ame answers, "will remember the names of some women who were spiritual guides. Their spirits have told me who is to be trained next."

Everyone chatters with anticipation.

Through a gap in the jungle of bodies around me I see Lah-ame hold his hand up for silence. "Our chief hunter will lead you away from the rough seas and into the safety of the jungle. There, as always, you will live together during the rainy season. But although I will leave to spend the season apart from the tribe, this time I will not be alone.

My apprentice will come with me. After I have taught her all that I know, she will return to the tribe and relearn her place among you. For, in the end, it is you who must accept her as your oko-jumu."

My people murmur with approval.

Again, Lah-ame holds up his hand to quiet the crowd. "The one whom I shall train to help the En-ge find the balance between old and new is Uido, the daughter of our chief hunter."

A great cheer rises from my people, and I feel their joy surging around me like a great tide. But Natalang says, "How long have you known?" I hear a stiffness in her voice.

"Since the strangers first came," I reply.

"You said nothing," she accuses. "Why did you not share this with me?"

"I wanted to," I say. "But I was afraid you would find me strange and would not want to be my friend anymore."

She opens her mouth to say something, but snaps it shut again.

"Forgive me." I reach out to touch her soft shoulder, but Natalang takes a step back.

Before I can say anything else, my family swallows me up. Mimi presses her cheek against mine. Then she lays her head on my shoulder and I feel my skin become wet with her tears. Tawai clings to her, a worried look on his face. But although I am sad to be leaving, I am too excited to weep.

Kara says, "I am honored you have chosen my daughter, Lah-ame." I see his chest is pushed out with pride.

Then Ashu's voice rises from the crowd. "Take me instead, Lah-ame. I am the strongest and fastest of anyone. And the best hunter." His words shock me. I cannot believe he wants to learn about spirits.

Lah-ame's reply is gentle. "I have no doubt you would work hard and well, Ashu. And you are indeed the best hunter among the boys. But I must be guided by the spirits in this matter."

"Give me a chance, Lah-ame," Ashu begs. "I will do anything you ask."

"I ask you to be a good brother to Uido," Lah-ame says. "The training is not easy. If she returns, she will need the love of her family."

Ashu presses his lips together in an angry line.

Mimi lifts her head from my shoulder. "The training, Uido. Will it cause pain? Are you not afraid?"

She looks so upset that I do not admit I am a little scared. Instead, I stroke her cheek and say, "My spirit has seen the Otherworld and it is beautiful, Mimi. So do not worry. I want nothing more than to learn from Lah-ame and would never be happy if you did not allow me to try."

Mimi holds me against her for a long while, then blows her breath across my cheeks. "Go well and return to us safely."

"Lah-ame should find someone else. I need you," Tawai whines. "Stay with us."

I hug Tawai as tightly as I can. When I let go, he bursts out crying and clings to Mimi again.

Danna comes up to us and pats Tawai's back. "Do not worry, Uido," he says to me. "I will take care of Tawai while you are gone." His face beams as he blows across my cheeks. "My spirit will be with yours until you return."

Kara hugs me next. "I know you will be successful. May Biliku-waye and Pulug-ame guide your spirit as you travel with Lah-ame."

Once he lets me go, my family steps aside to let the rest of the tribe say farewell. Women and men and elders and children and ra-gumul boys and girls all mix together like waves tumbling around me. People crowd in to breathe on my face and wish me safety and triumph on my journeys in the Otherworld.

But although I hear admiration in their voices and feel a comforting warmth in their breath, everyone seems to look at me differently now—almost as if I have suddenly turned into a stranger.

II

JOURNEY THROUGH THE OTHERWORLD

12

Lah-ame is silent as he leads me south. It is the same direction as the tribe's rainy season camp, but we take a different path through a part of the jungle where the undergrowth is so thick that I am sure no En-ge ever cut a trail. Lah-ame's feet move as easily as the wind over the spiky plants and thorny bushes. It is hard for me to keep up, although I carry nothing and Lah-ame carries a boar-skin water bag slung across his chest, a huge reed basket on his back and, as usual, his bulging medicine pouch, which dangles from his belt. Seeing Lah-ame always a few steps ahead, I feel nervous that I may never grow as strong as he is.

We walk all day, sipping frequently from Lah-ame's water bag, resting only for a short while when the sun is at its highest in the sky. At dusk we arrive near a small pool where Lah-ame tells me we will stop for the night. Lah-ame refills his water bag and gives me a few handfuls of nuts from his basket. I gulp them down, but when they are gone my stomach still feels empty.

"Hunger sharpens the senses," Lah-ame says, unfolding a leaf from his medicine bag. Inside is a greenish brown powder. "Do you know what this is, Uido?" he asks.

I guess it must be a curing powder of some kind, though I cannot tell by looking or sniffing at it. "May I taste it?"

Lah-ame taps out some powder onto my outstretched palm and mixes in a drop of water.

I rub the paste between my fingers, then lick it off. "It tastes like the drink you gave me for a stomachache once."

"You have a good memory." He points to a tree nearby that has a gray bark and pink flowers. "The stomach cure I gave you came from that beech tree's leaves. The juice of its stem will chase away pain in the joints. And the beech tree's leaves and bark can be made into poultices and splints to reduce swelling and cure broken bones."

Excitement washes away my hunger as I realize this is my first lesson.

Lah-ame reaches into his basket and hands me an empty lizard-skin bag. "Are you ready to start filling your pouch with medicine?"

My own medicine bag! I run the tips of my fingers over the scaly outside. Lah-ame waits patiently while I tie it to my waist belt, making four knots to be very certain it will not fall off.

"Now, Uido, bring me a handful of beech leaves." He lays two flat stones on the ground—the kind Mimi uses to grind ash and beeswax together to make glue.

It takes me a long time to grind the leaves into a paste smooth enough to satisfy Lah-ame. When I am finally done, he packs the medicine into a leaf and places it in my new medicine bag. I wonder what else it will hold and how soon it will be as full as Lah-ame's.

"Each oko-jumu's medicine bag is a little different, Uido," Lah-ame says as though he can hear my thoughts. He unties the pouch at his belt and hands it to me.

My fingers tingle with eagerness as I take the bag from him. Holding it as carefully as a bird's egg, I pull open the drawstring that holds the top closed. Inside, I glimpse healing objects and medicines: two pebbles, a few withered leaves and petals, many dried roots and many more leaf packets, bright purple seeds, several tiny pitchers covered with lids, and four white feathers from a sea eagle's belly. It delights me to think I will learn how to use all these cures.

Lah-ame lowers himself onto the uneven ground. Nearby, I stretch out my tired limbs. The soles of my feet hurt so much that I barely feel a thorn that pokes into the back of my thigh. My arms ache, too, from pounding and grinding my first medicine paste. Almost immediately I fall asleep.

For the next three days, we walk inland just as the tribe must be doing. On the way, Lah-ame sometimes points out a special plant or tree whose spirit can cure sickness. More often the medicines come from trees I already know but whose healing secrets were hidden from me.

At dusk on the fourth day, Lah-ame leads me to two leaf huts that sit under a laurel tree bursting with white flowers, just like the one behind his hut in our dry-season village. But these leaf huts have no walls—only rounded roofs that slope low to the ground—and they are made entirely of banana leaves, which are waxy enough to keep out the rain. Inside each hut is a bamboo sleeping platform, raised off the ground to keep us dry. Not far away, I hear a stream rumbling like my hungry stomach.

Our evening meal is a few handfuls of nuts and fruit, the same as the last three nights. I chew slowly, wondering what food the tribe is sharing tonight. By now the married women must be preparing a tasty meat stew, laughing and chattering as they cook.

Suddenly I miss everyone. Loneliness grips me by the throat so tightly that I cannot speak.

We sit together quietly, watching Pulug-ame hide the moon and stars behind the clouds he blows across the sky. After a while, Lah-ame points to one of the huts. "It is time to rest. Tomorrow I will help you travel to the Otherworld again."

A gentle drizzle begins to fall, wetting my skin. So I leave for the shelter of my new home. Soon after I lie on the sleeping platform, thunder booms through the dark night, making me wonder how Pulug-ame's voice sounds in the Otherworld.

I run my fingers across the smooth bones of my chaugata, imagining what it might feel like to hold hands with the spirits of my ancestors. Raindrops of excitement seem to leap within my belly just as they patter outside on the jungle floor.

13

The harsh cry of a sea eagle pulls me out of my night dream. I open my eyes and gaze at the banana-leaf roof. It takes a few moments to remember where I am.

"Uido," Lah-ame calls. I jump off the sleeping platform and rush to join him. A small drum is strapped to Lah-ame's chest and a bone rattle is knotted onto his chauga-ta.

"Follow me," is all he says as he strides toward the trees. The jungle is noisy with the songs of frogs celebrating the change of season. Thick knots of grass lick my feet, *whish, whish, whish, whish,* as I try to keep up with Lah-ame, wondering what he expects of me this morning.

We reach a part of the jungle where the air is heavy with the scent of ripe fruit. Lah-ame draws a circle on the ground with a twig.

"Lie down with your feet facing east and listen to my rattle and drum," he says. "Their sound will guide your spirit deeper into the Otherworld than it has gone before. After you have been there for a while, I will call you back with four sharp drumbeats."

I sink onto the mossy ground. The rattle sounds, followed by the drumbeat, but I am too excited to concentrate. I feel an ant's hair-thin legs tickling my skin and distracting me further. It wanders across the side of my neck, toward my earlobe. Afraid that it is a fire ant, I sit up and flick it off. My eyes meet Lah-ame's stern gaze.

"You did not even try!" he says.

"I am sorry," I mumble. "A *konoro-ta* was crawling up my face."

"Be attentive to your spirit, Uido. Leave your body here on the jungle floor."

I lie down again. The rattle begins—*tshh-tshh-tshh-tshh*—like falling leaves. The drum follows—*dha-dha-dha-dha*. *Tshh-tshh-tshh-tshh, dha-dha-dha-dha*. I try to make words out of the sounds. But the more I think, the darker my mind becomes. I count hundreds of drumbeats before giving up. I sit, pull my knees to my chest and hang my head in shame. "Why is it so hard today? I entered the Otherworld so easily on the cliff top and even forced my way in when I fought with Ashu."

Lah-ame sits on his haunches beside me. "The Otherworld is not a faraway place; it is just a different way to sense this world around us." He strokes my cheek. "Do not worry about how long it is taking. Allow your ear to drink in the sound of the rattle and the drum; use your spirit, not your body, to sense and feel."

Once more I lie back. The rattle begins again. This time I hear it say *shhhh* to the thoughts in my mind. Slowly my mind becomes still. Matching the drum's rhythm, I breathe deeply in and out. Then, all of a sudden, a bright light spreads behind my closed eyes.

The jungle disappears. I am standing by the edge of a pool. Warm sunshine pours across my shoulders and cool water slurps at my toes.

Welcome.

I spot a path leading away from the pool, with shoulder-high grasses on either side that seem to beckon me. I can still hear the drum as clearly as when I was in the jungle. So I dance along the path, keeping time with my feet. The tall grasses bend in and stroke me, like members of the tribe greeting a boy returning from his first hunt.

As I move farther away from the pool, the grass becomes shorter and the scent of vanilla flowers thickens the air. On the stem of a strange red-leafed plant, I see a large web hung with dew. It looks as though it were woven from strings of light. The spider at its center is no more than a black dot. In awe that such a little creature could create something so beautiful, I tremble. My spirit senses that I am in Biliku-waye's presence again. But this time she remains tiny, as though the slightest breath of wind could blow her away and destroy her web.

The drumbeat softens and I hear a whisper coming from near the plant that the spiderweb hangs on. When I bend down close, wanting to hear the voice a little better, I notice how unusual the plant is. It lacks flowers, but its leaves are as brightly colored as flowers' petals: red mottled with pink. The lower part of each leaf is shaped like the pitchers we use to store water, and the top part looks like a small lid.

I peer into one of the pitcher-shaped leaves. To my surprise, it is filled with sweet-smelling juice.

Just then, four sharp drumbeats cut into my mind.

I obey the call to return and trudge back down the path. A strong wind pushes at me, as though urging me to move faster. As soon as my feet splash into the pool again, all light disappears.

I open my eyes. It is a shock to find my body lying on the jungle floor, as though I never left.

"Well done, Uido." Lah-ame smiles.

"I saw Biliku-waye as a tiny spider. Why did she appear in such a delicate form?"

"Whenever your own spirit feels strong, the Other-worldly spirits will not appear large or terrifying." Lah-ame's smile widens. "Tell me on what plant Biliku-waye hung her web for you."

"The plant's leaves were shaped like water pitchers and filled with a sweet-smelling juice."

"That is the insect-eating plant," he says. "A creature that looks like a plant but acts like an animal. Its spirit is caught between two ways of living."

"How can a plant's spirit be like an animal's, Lah-ame? Plants are rooted to one place, while animals move. And there are so many other differences between them."

"This plant traps insects. But instead of catching them with a sticky tongue like a frog, the plant has a slippery leaf. Insects are fooled into thinking the brightly colored leaves are flower petals. If they try to land on the pitcher-shaped leaf and sip the juice inside, they slide down and drown in the juice instead. The plant then eats the insects just as an animal might."

"How do you know so much about this plant, Lah-ame? Have you seen it in the Otherworld, too?"

"It grows in this world, Uido."

"But where, Lah-ame? I have never heard anyone speak of it, nor have I seen it myself."

"One day you will," Lah-ame says. "If Biliku-waye hung her web on it in your vision, it means this is your special medicine plant. You must seek out this plant and bring its healing waters back to our people."

"When?" I ask, eager to see it again.

"Close to the end of your training." Lah-ame lays his hand on my shoulder as if he is trying to weigh down my curiosity. "That test is still far away, Uido."

I ask no more questions because I sense he will not answer them. But Lah-ame's refusal to speak about the last part of my training only makes me think all the more about the strange plant until I fall asleep that night.

14

From that day on I have hardly any time to wonder about where the insect-eating plant grows or how I must find it someday. Lah-ame keeps me busy learning new skills. I barely even have time to miss being with the rest of the tribe.

It is only at night, lying on my sleeping platform while rain slides off the banana-leaf roof, that I can think of them. I sometimes dream of being back in my tribe's circle of warmth. But if I see or hear the strangers' flying boats during the day, I have a terrible dream at night—of Ragavan visiting the island, cutting down our jungle and taking Tawai away in his boat. Yet when I wake, the steady downpour and the *hhhhffff* of the stormy wind comforts and reminds me that the strangers cannot land on our shores in the rainy season.

Most mornings Lah-ame and I gather plant and animal parts that have healing powers. Then we return to the shelter of our banana-leaf huts and roast or squeeze or grind what we collected to make medicines. I enjoy feeling the growing weight of my lizard-skin pouch.

In the evenings, after our meal of berries and fruit and

nuts, my stomach often growls with hunger. But in the darkness, Lah-ame teaches me many things. I learn how to find and chase away the lau that cause disease by entering a person's body and capturing the spirit; the chants an oko-jumu must say to thank the spirits for fire, good weather, and successful hunts; the rituals that celebrate birth and marriage; and all the tales of our people. He guides me farther and farther into the Otherworld with his rattle and drum. But although I learn to journey there with ease, I never again see the insect-eating plant.

Then, four moons after we parted from the rest of the tribe, Lah-ame gives me my first test. At dawn he begins to ask me about all he has taught. My voice does not falter once and I answer every question correctly. When the sky beyond the mat of branches above us grows dark, Lah-ame finally stops.

"I am pleased by how quickly you learned about healing," he says. "Tomorrow I will teach you how to make fire."

His praise lifts my spirit like a breeze, until I feel like I am floating above the treetops with joy. That night I dream of kindling a great orange blaze while my entire tribe watches in admiration.

The next day, Lah-ame brings me his fire tools. He places a trunk with a small hollow carved in the middle on the ground, under the shelter of his roof. I kneel beside it, as I have seen him do, and place his long fire stick inside the hollow. He helps me run the vine rope across the fire stick and shows me how to balance the stick inside the hollow while churning it with the vine rope. I am surprised how difficult it is. My palms redden and blister as the rope cuts into my skin. It takes me eight days to build up the skill and strength to move the rope fast enough while keeping the fire stick in place. By then the hollow in the trunk is as black as my hair and my palms are rough as bark. On the evening of the eighth day, I finally see a burst of gray smoke. But that is just the first step.

I learn that I must keep going after the smoke appears, until sparks finally fly, then blow on the sparks to keep them alive and feed them quickly with bark strips before the sparks go out. Next, I must use the strips to light a pile of twigs and leaves. Only when this pile is alight can I feed the blaze with large branches.

After four more days of trying and failing, Lah-ame says, "Remember, everything has a spirit. To create fire, you must bring together the power of the trees' spirits and use this along with the strength of your own spirit and body."

Before trying again, I pray softly to the trees from which the firewood came. Then I churn the fire stick in the hollow with my vine rope. When I see the first sparks, I reach for a handful of bark strips as usual. But this time, instead of worrying about whether they will catch, I imagine my spirit as a steady light, pulling the sparks toward the bark strips.

The Otherworld is within everything; as much inside this fire as outside it.

As soon as the strips are alight, I use them to set fire to a pile of twigs nearby. While I stoke the blaze with more twigs and branches, Lah-ame puts the hollowed-out trunk, vine rope and fire stick away. Soon my fire is not just crackling but roaring.

As I watch my fire grow larger, my spirit swells with a feeling of triumph. Although my back and arms ache from days of hunching over the fire tools, I wish my tribe were here to dance with me around the flames I built.

"Have you not forgotten something?" Lah-ame says.

"Have I?" I ask.

Lah-ame rises and says a prayer of thanks to Pulug-ame, who gave the gift of fire to our ancestors. Ashamed that I forgot to thank him myself, I bow my head and repeat the words after Lah-ame. We sit on the warm earth, close to the fire.

"Uido, I, too, was overjoyed the first time I made fire," Lah-ame says. "I made the same mistake you did. It is only natural. But the more dangerous mistake even an older oko-jumu may repeat is to enjoy one's power too much."

"Sorry," I mumble.

For a long time, Lah-ame squeezes my temples, until my heady pride at making the fire drains out of me. "A fire like the one you just made has the power to warm us, light up our nights and cook our food. But if left unguarded, it can leap into a rage and burn down a village. And just as you learn to control the fire's power by tending to it with skill and respect, so must you watch yourself, Uido. Spirits may use their powers to punish and destroy; we must not. If you become oko-jumu someday, your every act and decision must be for the tribe's good."

"I will remember, Lah-ame." I stare into the flames and hug my knees to my chest. After days of churning the fire stick with a vine rope, my arm muscles bulge out like a young man's.

"Your training is nearly complete," Lah-ame says.

"Not already?" I say.

Lah-ame smiles at my surprise.

"Tomorrow we will start making a canoe, to help you with the final test that awaits."

"A canoe?" This confuses me. "Is it not far too stormy to go out on the ocean for another two moons at least?"

Lah-ame points to the west. "You will need to canoe up the stream and search the swamp until you find your insect-eating plant."

"It grows in the swamp?" I try to keep my voice from shaking. I cannot believe Lah-ame will send me there. I was about ten seasons old when Kara and three of his best hunters left to see what was in the western part of our island. Only one of his hunters returned with him.

They told of walking west until they came to a place where the mud stank of dead leaves. There they found crocodiles: creatures three times as long as a grown man, with teeth sharper than a shark's. These *duku-ta* hid in the mud, pretending to be dead tree trunks, until a man came near enough for them to gulp down. Kara killed the crocodile that ate two of our men and carried it back. But though its giant body fed the entire tribe, Kara warned us all to keep far away from the swamp and he never went there again.

"Once your canoe is made, I will take you to the swamp," Lah-ame says. "But you must journey through it alone. The insect-eating plant's waters will carry special healing powers in your hands, and you will need these waters to heal. It also holds a message to help you guide the tribe into the future, a message that you might only understand long after you complete your journey."

That evening, I hardly taste the food we eat. Even with the fire I built dancing in front of me and my medicine bag at my waist, I feel unprepared for such a test. Although the crackling flames warm my skin, my spirit remains cold with horror. Lah-ame stays close by until I leave for my own hut, but we find nothing more to say and his presence no longer comforts me.

15

That night, I am unable to rest on my sleeping platform. My body feels as tense as a tightly pulled bowstring. I twist and untwist my medicine bag's drawstring between my fingers, wondering if the tribe's warm breath will ever stroke my cheeks again. I long to feel Mimi's and Tawai's arms around me and hear Danna say I will survive whatever lies ahead.

It would help me so much to even glimpse them from a distance. Perhaps I could try to see them in spirit at least, using my power to journey through the Otherworld.

Lah-ame is fast asleep. Except for my spirit's wanderings in dreams, he has always been near me when I entered the Otherworld. I remember his warning after my dream of snakes not to send my spirit away from my body without his guidance until my training was complete. But I must search with my spirit for my tribe's communal hut tonight, because I cannot bear my loneliness any longer.

I slip out into the jungle. As soon as I am out of Lah-ame's sight, I lie on the moist earth facing east and close my eyes. Listening to the wind rattling the leaves overhead and raindrops drumming on the jungle floor, I send my spirit into the Otherworld.

Behind my closed eyes, I see a light twinkling like a firefly in the trees. I drift over the moist earth toward it. It leads me to a moonlit clearing, where I see a huge banana-leaf hut with a roof sloping low to the ground and no walls. Moving closer, I see my entire tribe asleep inside. Family groups are huddled together on the many wooden platforms. Natalang's thighs wobble as she turns on her side, next to her mimi. The tips of Danna's mouth are turned up as though he is having a good dream.

Across from Danna's family lies my own. Tawai's head rests against Mimi's shoulder. Her long fingers are wrapped around Kara's thick ones but Ashu's fists are clenched even in his sleep.

My chest tightens with loneliness. I am still far enough away that I can only see them. I want to get near enough to smell the sweat on Kara's skin, hear Mimi's breath rising and falling like the ocean waves, feel the warmth of Tawai's hand curled up inside mine.

I imagine waking them up and hearing the tribe's shouts—first of surprise, then of welcome. But if I return to my people now, it will be harder than ever to leave again. Knowing that I must journey through the swamp, I might not find the strength to pull myself away. It feels very long ago that my spirit was so full of excitement and curiosity about the Otherworld that Lah-ame's warnings of pain and death meant little to me.

Slowly I force myself to glide out of our communal hut and into the clearing. The huge leaf hut grows small and distant as I leave it behind and float back across the jungle. When I turn for one last look, it has become as tiny as a spider's web.

Opening my eyes, I find myself alone once more, raindrops sparkling around me in the moonlight.

I return to my lonely banana-leaf hut. When I fall asleep, I dream of seeing my tribe again as if from a great distance. The faces and bodies of my people blur together in my mind, all growing into one person. I see this person's spirit as a bright glow, but as I move toward it, the glow shrinks into a dot no larger than a little spider. Frightened, I reach out my hand. As the bright spot climbs into my palm, I understand that this delicate spirit is mine to protect. For a moment at least, I am not afraid of what awaits me; instead, I fear only for the tribe whose safety I will hold in my hands if I become oko-jumu.

16

When I awake, I feel refreshed and determined to find the insect-eating plant. I must collect its healing waters and learn what it has to say—for the sake of my people. If going through the swamp will give me knowledge to help guide the En-ge into the future, then I must do it.

Later that morning, Lah-ame goes into the jungle with me to choose a tree trunk for a canoe. It takes us nearly half the day in the pouring rain just to drag the trunk back to my leaf hut. He shows me how to carve out the trunk using his stone adze. While I work, he sings stories of how our ancestors used waves and currents, as well as the movements of birds and stars, to guide them from island to island in days long gone. I do not understand why I need to learn any of this since I will never need to canoe far into the ocean. But I am glad to learn something new because it keeps me from worrying about the upcoming journey. Lah-ame keeps me up late into the night, naming the stars that help the En-ge keep direction.

For the rest of the rainy season I continue to hollow out the log canoe while Lah-ame teaches me many things. I learn how an oko-jumu must predict the change of seasons by watching the patterns drawn across the sky and sea and the behavior of the plant and animal spirits. In the evenings I practice fire making and at night Lah-ame tells me more about canoeing across the ocean. His songs and stories feed my body as well as my spirit. My back and shoulders grow broader still from hitting stone against wood, and my spirit's determination to pass the test ahead strengthens as well.

By the time the canoe is carved, along with two poles and paddles, the wind and rain have weakened. On the morning after the moon has grown into a circle for the sixth time since we left the tribe, Lah-ame says, "Tomorrow we will set out."

We spend much of the day preparing for when I reach the swamp. Lah-ame gives me many empty wooden vessels with lids.

"These are to store the waters from your special medicine plant," he says.

That night, I keep my thoughts on the image of my tribe sleeping together in the communal hut. It helps me stay determined to find the insect-eating plant and ignore my fear of the swamp.

Lah-ame wakes me at dawn. I knot my medicine bag to my waist belt with two vine ropes, to make very sure it will not fall off. We pile everything we need for the journey into my canoe and heave it onto our shoulders. The canoe is heavy, but I lift it with ease. My footsteps are steady as we walk to the stream. We lower the canoe into the cold, mist-covered water.

"You have a new strength this morning," Lah-ame remarks. "This is good, because there is a new skill to learn today." He leaps into the front end of the canoe. "Watch what I do." I hear monkeys screeching with curiosity in the treetops as Lah-ame pushes off the bottom of the stream with a pole.

Lah-ame shows me how to use the paddle. I am amazed how easily this skill comes to me—as though I have been canoeing since my childhood. The monkeys follow us, swinging from the trees along the bank for a time. Their happy chatter encourages me. But soon the canoe is too fast for them to keep up. I am sorry when we leave them behind.

As evening approaches, we lose the distant chatter of monkeys, then the songs of birds and finally even the chirp of crickets. I hear only the splash of our poles in the creek, the *plip-tup-plip-tup* of rain and water slapping at the sides of our canoe. Tall trees no longer stand guard on the stream's banks, which turn muddy. Plants with twisted trunks grow out of the mud, their branches hanging out across the water as though they were reaching for me.

"What plants are those?" My finger shakes as I point at them.

"These are mangrove trees," Lah-ame says. "Their roots jut out of the ground to help them breathe."

I watch the sun setting behind the mangroves ahead of us. The stream becomes narrower and clouds of mosquitoes swarm around my ears, *Zzzzt, Zzzzt,* they drone, biting into my cheeks, my arms, my back, my front. The stench of rotting leaves fills the air.

Lah-ame gets out of the canoe and pulls it up a clay bank. I hear something thrashing in the water behind us and glance back. Through the fading light, I see the jaw of a huge lizard snapping shut and sinking beneath the water.

I clamber up the slippery bank as fast as I can. "Is that a duku-ta?"

"You are afraid, Uido," Lah-ame says.

I want to deny it, but my voice has given me away already. I have nothing with which to defend myself—not even a digging stick.

"There are many crocodiles here," Lah-ame says. "But all creatures can be calmed by a true healer." He hands me his bone rattle. My fingers tremble as I take it. The rattle makes a pleasant sound, like flowing water. I knot it tightly to my bone necklace but I do not see how it will be of any use in fighting a crocodile.

Next, Lah-ame slips a water bag over one of my shoulders and a bag filled with food over the other. "It is time for me to leave," he says.

Although I know the journey through the swamp must be mine alone, I have pushed this moment of parting out of my mind, refusing to think of it. Now it is here, I can get no words out.

"Your spirit and body have grown powerful, Uido, powerful enough for you to sense your way through the Otherworld alone and return safely to our people." Lah-ame holds my face in his hands for a long moment. "May Biliku-waye and Pulug-ame guide you as you walk north to find your special medicine and learn the plant's message."

He blows across my cheeks, then walks down the bank to the canoe.

I watch Lah-ame push away into the gloom. My spirit feels trapped, as if in a bad dream from which I cannot awake.

The ripples made by Lah-ame's boat slowly fade.

And there is only silence.

17

I peer into the swamp ahead as the darkness thickens around me. A tangle of mangrove roots sticks out of the ground like the legs of a gigantic spider. It makes me think of Biliku-waye.

Praying she will guide me safely through this place, I take a step toward the spiderlike roots, away from the water and the crocodiles. Behind me, I hear the squelch of mud.

I cannot help looking back. A crocodile four times my size is clambering onto the bank, dragging its tail across the wet earth.

Panic rises like cold water in my chest. Not far ahead, I see a circular patch of mud between the mangrove trees. It looks unnaturally smooth—like the strangers' metal boats. Thinking it will be easier to escape the crocodile if I am running over mud than if I am stumbling across mangrove branches, I run toward the mud as fast as the swampy ground will allow.

A fallen tree trunk blocks my way. I stumble over it. But then the log comes alive. Another crocodile!

I leap away.

When I land, my feet sink ankle-deep into the smooth mud. I try to go forward, but I only slide in deeper. The mud sucks hungrily at my legs, pulling me down. In no time it rises up to my knees, my thighs.

The crocodiles hang back from the gleaming mud, their unblinking eyes shining in the light of the rising moon. I slap and kick at the mud but the earth's grip tightens. The more I struggle, the lower I sink. I fall in up to my waist. The stench of mud fills my nose and my throat feels dry, as though there is no water left inside me.

I hear a voice through the gloom.

Why are you here?

I shiver.

Why are you here?

"To find the insect-eating plant," I whisper.

Why do you want to find it?

Closing my eyes, I picture that strange, beautiful creature again—the pink-red of its pitcher-shaped leaves, the sweet-smelling juice inside. It feels so long ago when I first saw it, my spirit filled with no more than curiosity and wonder. "I want to learn the plant's message and carry its healing waters with me," I say.

Why?

In my mind I see again, as from a distance, the huge communal hut shrinking, all my people coming together as one person. The image calms me. "I hope its message will guide us into a safe future. And it is my special medicine plant, whose powers will help me care for my people, whom I love."

If you act lovingly, the earth spirit will let you go. Stop kicking and slapping at Tarai-mimi. Why are you hurting her?

I shake my head, confused. Then I realize that in the last few moments, while being still, I sank no deeper into the mud.

With all my strength, I try to control my body's urge to fight its way out. Carefully, I feel for the rattle around my neck and move it back and forth to calm my spirit. The crocodiles, too, seem calmed by the sound. They stop staring at me and instead gaze up at the moon. A sudden gust of wind cools the sweat on my forehead. I lift my chin up to the night sky and breathe in deeply.

Listening to the watery sound of the rattle, I imagine it is not mud around my body but a stream. Instead of struggling against the earth's grip, I pretend I am wading through shallow water. The mud squelches with every movement, but its hold on me weakens.

Slowly, slowly, I get closer to the edge of the stinking pit. Just beyond the gleaming mud, I see the dark shape of a mangrove tree. Its spidery roots help keep the trunk above the swampy ground, and I hope they are strong enough to hold me too.

I reach out and grab the roots. Little by little I pull myself up. My fingers curl higher around the roots, then around the lowest part of the trunk. At last, hugging tightly to the tree, I heave my body out of the pit.

More mangrove trees grow in the swampy ground ahead. I crawl deep into the tangle of gnarled roots. When

I dare to look back through the darkness, the crocodiles are gone and the sticky mud is no more than a faint gleam.

But my bags of food and water are lost—they must have slipped off my shoulder and fallen into the pit. Thankfully, my medicine bag still hangs at my waist—although it is covered with mud. I pull open the drawstring and see by the moonlight that squeezes through the mangrove branches that everything inside is clean. Bowing my head, I say a grateful prayer to Biliku-waye.

My stomach growls with hunger as I lie back in the nest of mangrove roots. They poke into my back and a thick mat of thirsty mosquitoes settles down on top of me. Hearing a rustle in the leaves overhead, I look up to see a viper slithering up the branch. Yet despite the snake, the mosquitoes and my hunger, I smile in triumph. After making my way safely past the crocodiles and getting out of the sucking mud alive, it feels like nothing could stop me from finding the insect-eating plant. I hug my own strong body, tired but happy to be alive. And although it is uncomfortable, I fall asleep among the roots.

18

The next morning, I wake up late, feeling almost as tired as when I went to sleep. The sun has climbed into the middle of the sky and the heat has chased the mosquitoes away. The viper, too, is gone. But my stomach is so empty it hurts, and my tongue is as dry as a withered leaf. I desperately need a drink of water.

I poke in between the mangrove roots and pull up a handful of wet mud. Holding it above my mouth, I squeeze hard. Brown water drips onto my lips but it tastes so bad that I spit it out.

Looking around me, I try to decide what to do next. My body is bumpy and swollen from mosquito bites. But as soon as I picture the insect-eating plant in my mind again, I realize something that gives me new strength: the plant has watery juice for me to drink.

I gaze ahead, through the closely woven tree trunks. To the north, I spot a patch of red. Hoping the insect-eating plants grow there, I crawl across the mangrove roots in that direction.

Soon I am forced to leave the shelter of the trees behind. Wet mud stretches in front of me, broken only by pools of brown water. I break off a mangrove branch and walk forward carefully, testing the ground ahead with every step. Mud squelches between my toes and leeches wriggle up my legs. I have seen a few leeches by our pool with Natalang, but never as many as in this swamp. I stop to flick the ugly creatures off my legs and continue north, toward the reddish patch.

As I move closer, my eyes make out the pitcher-shaped leaves. For a few moments, I do not dare to let myself rejoice, afraid that it is just my imagination. But the plants do not disappear as I approach them.

Though my skin burns and my head aches, I rush forward as fast as I can until I am surrounded by the insect-eating plants. I sink down on my knees among them and take a deep breath of the sweet-smelling air.

Drink.

I tear off a leaf and swallow all the juice inside. Leaf after leaf I suck dry, until my throat is soothed and my thirst is gone. Even my stomach feels full.

"Thank you," I whisper.

Rub the leaves onto your body.

Like a snake shedding its old skin, I scrape off the dried mud still on me. Then I crush some leaves in my palm and smear them over myself. To my surprise, the pain in the bumps left by the mosquitoes lessens. When I rub the juice into my temples, my head stops aching.

"This juice works faster than any of the medicines in my pouch," I say, surprised by how refreshed I feel. "Why?"

Think back to what brought you here today.

"I saw the insect-eating plants in my first vision of the Otherworld."

And when did your spirit first enter the Otherworld?

"The day the strangers came. But . . . but they make me angry."

Their ways also make you curious.

I think of the strangers' fast metal boat and the wonderful paintings inside Ragavan's box. Unable to deny that the strangers' magic amazes me, I remain silent.

It is not wrong to be curious. The strangers are different, not evil.

Remembering the disturbing aura around Ragavan's head, I disagree. "If the strangers are not evil, why does Lah-ame want to keep us far away from them?"

Lah-ame loves the way of the oko-jumu and the world of the En-ge. He brought your tribe to this island to protect them, like an eagle who builds a nest high up on a cliff to keep its eggs safe. But as every eagle knows, the eggs will hatch. And one day the young must grow wings and fly away.

"We have everything we need here," I say. "None of us wants to leave the island."

Maybe not yet. But this island is small and the ocean is large.

"The Otherworld is larger."

Few spirits travel to the Otherworld as willingly as yours.

I nod, thinking of how uninterested Natalang was in the Otherworld—and yet how fascinated she was by the fruit that the strangers brought from across the sea.

Once, long ago, this swamp was part of the jungle. Then it turned into a swamp. Most plants found it hard to live through the change. But the insect-eating plants survived because they learned how to eat insects, just as animals do. And yet their spirits remain deeply rooted in the ways of plants. Somehow they held on to the beauty of plant life and took from animals only that which made them stronger. To live in their new world, they had to find a balance between the ways of animals and plants.

"What does all that mean?" I ask. "How will this knowledge help me guide the tribe?"

One day you may understand. But no one can ever tell you how to overcome the many tests that lie ahead.

"Where should I go now?" I try not to sound disappointed, and yet I cannot help wishing the plants had something more for me—like a prayer or a magical object that would keep the strangers away from our island forever.

Walk northeast for four days. By night on the fourth day, you will reach the cliff that stretches across the north of the island. Climb the rocks and you will find your oko-jumu waiting at the top. Take as many leaves and as much juice as you can to feed yourself and to heal your people in times of need.

From my medicine bag, I take out the empty wooden vessels that Lah-ame gave me. Carefully, I pinch off many leaves and drain every drop of juice into my vessels. I fill them all and place the leaves in my pouch.

The sooner you start walking, the sooner your journey will end.

"I thank you," I say, picking up my mangrove branch again. My spirit feels so calm and soothed in the plants' presence that it is hard to leave them behind. Yet I am also eager to see Lah-ame again and celebrate my successful journey with him.

Remembering what Lah-ame taught me about keeping direction by looking at the sun, I start walking northeast.

At each step, I test the ground ahead with my branch, although I see no more pits of hungry mud. The juice of the insect-eating plants swells in my stomach, which feels as heavy as if it were filled with meat. And although my ears are irritated by the *zzzt, zzzt* of mosquitoes, the juice works better than fresh body paint to keep both them and the leeches away.

Slowly, the ground underfoot becomes firmer. Glad not to have mud squelching between my toes, I move faster. By sunset, I see short trees poking up into the sky. They are not as tall or as thick as in our jungle, but it feels good to see them and better still to leave the stink of the swamp behind. I stop and rest beneath a tree for the night.

The next morning, Pulug-ame sends a gentle drizzle. I hold my mouth open to the sky and let the sweet water moisten my tongue and trickle down my throat. Over the next two days, the rain gets even lighter. I wonder if the tribe, too, is walking back up the island or if they have returned to the dry-season village already.

Late in the morning on the fourth day, I see the cliff rising up like a distant wall. My footsteps quicken and I reach the foot of the cliff at twilight. Holding my rattle high above my head, I shake it in celebration.

A new burst of strength gushes into my tired limbs at the thought that I will soon be with Lah-ame again. "I, Uido, found the insect-eating plant and I carry its healing waters!" I sing out, although there is nobody to hear me. My feet kick at the ground in a dance of joy and my triumphant spirit seems to leap as high as the cliff.

19

Eager to be back with Lah-ame, I start up the cliff path.
The clay is smooth but not slippery and it smells pleasant,
like wet body paint.

A short while later, in the moonlit darkness, I reach
the top of the cliff. I suck in a long stream of air, enjoying
the salty taste I know so well. A soft wind kisses my bare
skin as if in welcome as I listen to the familiar song of the
ocean far beneath me.

Although Lah-ame is not yet here, I sense that he will
come soon. Too tired to go any farther, I lie down on my
back, drenching my body in a great pool of moonlight.

When I awake, midday sunshine pours across the ground
and Lah-ame is standing near me. "Welcome back, Uido,"
he says. "From the very beginning of your training I knew
you would succeed."

He reaches down and pulls me into his arms. His
breath is a calm breeze on my face and I feel his spirit
glowing with pride and happiness.

"Thank you for your guidance, Lah-ame," I say,
though the words seem too small. I can only hope he
senses the depth of my gratitude.

"So," he says, letting me go, "your training with me is almost at an end. There is just one last thing. Uido, would you like to fly?" He runs his hand over his white curls and pulls out one of the four feathers tucked into his head-band. "The sea eagle is my spirit animal, Uido. And I will ask that he let you fly with him one time so that someday, when you meet your spirit animal, you will have a sense of how to send your spirit into its body."

To fly with an eagle sounds more wonderful than any-thing I ever imagined. The thought of it sets my heart skipping like sunshine on water.

Lah-ame faces east and raises his hands. The tips of his fingers seem to touch the clouds. "Kolo-ame," he calls, "come to me."

I see an eagle appear in the east. The bird streaks to-ward us across the blue, carried by a sudden rush of wind from far across the sea. It hovers above us. Looking up, I see its soft white belly and the dark tips of its great wings.

"Brother, this is Uido," Lah-ame says to the eagle. "She has walked a long way with me and hopes to become an oko-jumu. Will you take her upon your shoulders?"

The eagle screeches.

Lah-ame leads me to the edge of the cliff. We stop barely a hand's width from where the rock drops straight down into the water. Lah-ame spreads my arms out to my sides. "Close your eyes."

I stand on tiptoe. Lah-ame lets go of me and I feel a spurt of fear.

"Allow your body to become as light as an eagle's feather." Lah-ame's whisper is the voice of the wind tugging at my feet. "Let the eagle's sight fill your eyes."

I feel an eagle's feather stroke across the tip of my outstretched fingers. I feel the air entering my body, cool and fresh.

I am on the eagle's back, hearing the beat of its wings. Below us, my island shines, the jungle as green as a parrot's feathers.

We swoop low over the cliff, eastward along the island's edge, until we are at the tall rock that marks the highest point on the island. Then we fly above the steep jungle path that leads down from the cliffs to the wide expanse of our beach along the eastern shore.

We turn inward, dipping beneath the trees that separate the beach from our dry-season village. There, over the clearing, we hover for a few moments, watching the women at work below. I see Mimi and her youngest sister sitting close to our hut, weaving a basket from strips of cane. She looks up as we swoop down and I wonder if her spirit senses my presence close to her. At the edge of the village, between the circle of huts and the jungle, a few children are swinging on a vine. Tawai is with them, taller since I last saw him, but no fatter. I hear his happy shouts before we rise high up again, above the treetops.

Away we soar toward the south of our island, passing over the huts where Lah-ame and I stayed in the rainy season and above the large communal hut where my tribe was living. Far to the west, I glimpse the mangrove swamp. We glide back, north and east, over the waves of our fishing beach where the strangers came ashore.

The strangers' island lies in a straight line from here.

I gaze down at the white flecks dotting the blue sea. It is dusk as we fly further east, away from my island, until through the darkness I see a beach I recognize—where Lah-ame's friend stood in my vision on the cliff long ago. All night, we fly among the stars. But at dawn, I hear the eagle screech four times as though to call me out of the Otherworld. I float down through the pink sky like an eagle feather. My feet grow heavy again and my toes feel the earth beneath them.

I open my eyes and see the eagle perched on Lah-ame's shoulder.

"Well done, Uido." His eyes twinkle.

I reach out to the eagle but it turns away. I withdraw my hand, feeling a little hurt.

Lah-ame says gently, "This is my brother, Uido."

"But he carried me. Is he not my spirit animal now too?"

Lah-ame shakes his head. "He only did what I requested, Uido. Someday you will find your own spirit animal—one that you may touch and call and speak to at any time."

"What kind of animal is it, Lah-ame?"

"I sense yours is a water spirit, unlike mine."

"Must I seek it, like my special medicine plant?" I ask.

"Your spirit animal will seek you out," he replies. "It

will challenge you to a fight. And either it will kill you or else you will win and the animal's spirit will become a reflection of yours."

"I do not understand, Lah-ame. What does it mean to win over its spirit?"

"Your spirit animal is a guide whom you can call upon for help. You may send your spirit into its body, just as you can send your spirit through the Otherworld. When you do so, you will sense everything through your spirit animal and travel with it. And your spirit animal's wisdom may help you lead the tribe."

At these words, the eagle screeches and takes flight again.

Lah-ame turns to face the rising sun and bows his head. "Biliku-waye, Pulug-ame, I thank you for guiding Uido on the spirit paths and I ask you to protect her when she meets her spirit animal. May she always carry not only our songs and stories and medicines and memories, but also the happiness of each day on these islands."

"Lah-ame, may I rejoin the tribe now?" For a moment I worry that I sound ungrateful.

Lah-ame places his palms on my shoulders. "You learned faster than I expected. But the air of the cliff top is light, Uido. Here it is easy to balance the worlds of spirit and flesh. Once you are back in the village with the others, it will be hard to keep your mind clear enough to enter the Otherworld and let the spirits visit you. The most dangerous part of your oko-jumu training lies ahead, not behind."

I try to stifle the impatient sigh that rises to my lips, hoping he will let me go soon.

Instead, he continues, "And one final warning: until you meet your spirit animal, you will not have the strength to heal someone else on your own. If you try to heal another person before this happens, you will endanger yourself and shake the tribe's faith in our ways."

Lah-ame blows his breath across my face and hands me a bag of water. "Go well, Uido. I will follow later."

My spirit is so full of anticipation at meeting my tribe again that I barely listen to Lah-ame's warnings. I thank him, tighten the knot that holds my medicine bag in place and blow across his cheeks. My breath feels shallow, as though I am already running home.

20

As I race away from Lah-ame, the wind blows a fresh strength into my body. I leap across the stones in my path, eager to be surrounded by my tribe again. I do not rest for long, even during the hottest part of the day, because I feel cooled just thinking of the shady trees surrounding our village.

I near the village at dusk. In the fading light, the joy I felt earlier weakens, and I remember that my tribe looked at me like I was a stranger only moments after Lah-ame announced that I was to be his apprentice. My steps falter and I worry about how my people will treat me now. But even as I slow down, a ra-gumul boy sees me and cries out, "*Olaye, olaye, odo-lay, odo-lay!* Come, everyone! Uido is back!"

He races up to me, sits cross-legged on the jungle floor and holds his hands out, waiting to take me in his lap the way our tribe always welcomes someone who has been gone a long time. With relief, I collapse into his lap.

"Uido!" Danna bursts out of the trees and pulls me to my feet. His face is as round as ever, his smile still as wide. But he is much taller. Fresh scars run across his upper arms and thighs. He has cut a beautiful pattern of lines and dots into his own skin, but seeing his tattoo upsets me because it means I missed my best friend's manhood ceremony.

Danna breathes across my face. I notice that his mouth has a pleasant scent like earth moistened by the first rain.

He sits and draws me onto his lap. I shift awkwardly, sensing his rock-hard legs beneath mine. It feels different from sitting on the other boy's lap moments ago. The Danna I knew was a boy; the one who holds me now is a man.

"I missed you." His voice has deepened into a man's voice as well. He pinches my waist gently. "You have grown muscles." The pebble-smooth skin of his chest presses against the full length of my back. My body trembles as if a cool breeze has wrapped itself around me instead of Danna's warm arms. "And you have also grown very silent." He holds my chin and turns my face to meet his.

His eyes look just as warm and caring as before—and it comforts me to see that they, at least, have not changed. I let my fingers wander over the scars on his shoulder. "Does the tattoo still hurt?"

"Not at all. Do you like it?" He sounds anxious to hear my approval.

"Yes, very much."

Tawai tumbles into my lap, interrupting us. I hug him, but he quickly wriggles out of my arms, jumps up and takes me by the hand. Danna takes the other and together they drag me closer to our village. "*Olaye, olaye, odo-lay, odo-lay!* Uido is here again!" Their shouts are echoed by other voices.

Kara strides over to us, exclaiming, "We did not expect you back for another season at least!"

"Lah-ame said I learned faster than he imagined possible," I tell him.

"I am so proud of you, Uido." He lifts me onto his shoulders and carries me to the center of the clearing before he sets me down on his lap.

A fire is already lit and I smell roast boar and turtle stew. I take a deep gulp of air, swallowing the wonderful scent of cooking as men, women and elders buzz around me like bees on a hive. "Welcome back, Uido!" "How much bigger you have grown!" "Where is Lah-ame?"

I feel the joyous thump of Mimi's heart as she clutches me tightly and pats my cheeks with her slender fingers. "You are thin as a twig!" she says, blind to the muscles bulging on my arms and legs. "Did Lah-ame feed you nothing at all?"

"But Mimi," I say, "the training was wonderful. Truly."

"We must fatten you up," she says. "I will see to that."

Kara folds me and Mimi in his arms, while Tawai squeezes himself in between our legs. It feels wonderful to have my family wrapped around me, until I realize that Ashu has not joined us. Nor has Natalang greeted me yet. As my people pass me from lap to lap, I search for the two of them among the crowd.

At last, Natalang bounces over. She remains standing, but I am so happy to see her that I jump up. "You are not still angry with me, are you?" I ask.

"No," she replies, but she makes no gesture of affection that shows we are friends. "Welcome back, Uido."

I feel stung by her stiff tone. I want to say something to make it all right again between us, but she steps away and one of Kara's hunters snatches me up in his lap.

Then I see Ashu, sitting close to the bachelor hut. Like Danna, Ashu wears the scars of manhood now. He does not look up from the bone knife he is sharpening with a piece of *tolma* crystal. But I refuse to be angry with him. I break away from the others, run toward him and put a hand on his back.

Ashu keeps chipping at the bone knife, pretending he does not notice my touch. His body feels hot, and I sense his resentment smoldering like the embers of a fire.

"Ashu?" I say.

Without a word, he pulls away and stalks off into the darkness of the jungle.

Mimi comes up to me.

"Why does Ashu hate me so much?" I ask her.

"Perhaps he is a little jealous, Uido."

"Of what? My time with Lah-ame was not all easy."

"You must not let him upset you. Come." Mimi takes my hand and leads me back to the others. "The food is ready."

Mimi sits with me, making sure I eat a lot. It is so good to feel meat on my tongue again. I linger over each bite. And even better than the taste of the meat is the feeling of sharing and eating together with my tribe again.

Ashu returns to join the circle, but sits far away from us. Everyone else—Tawai most of all—crowds around, asking about where Lah-ame took me and what we did together. I tell them some of the stories I learned from Lah-ame about our tribe's past—but nothing about my walks on the spirit paths, worried that speaking of this would push my people away and make them feel I have grown strange. When I ask about all that has happened while I was away, everyone is happy to gossip and I to listen.

After we clean our hands and teeth, Kara pours the embers from the fire into torches to keep it alive because Lah-ame still has not returned to the village. For an instant, I want to tell him that he does not need to because I can start a new fire now. But I say nothing, unsure if it is my place yet to start fire for the tribe.

When he is finished with the fire, Kara brings out Lah-ame's drum and beats a dance rhythm in celebration of my return. In a few moments, everyone is either singing or dancing or else slapping their palms against their thighs to show how happy they are to see me again. Danna pulls me onto my feet and into the circle of dancers. Natalang's oldest sister makes a place for us, throwing an arm lightly across my shoulders. Yet I hardly feel her touch with Danna close by me. I slide my hand around his sturdy waist, savoring the new feelings that ripple inside me every time we are so close.

Outside the bachelor hut, I see Natalang and Ashu sitting together. He tucks a red hibiscus flower behind her ear with a tenderness I never thought Ashu could have.

"Is that my brother?" I say. "With Natalang?"

Danna laughs. "Love makes even the fiercest hunters gentle."

"Love?" I stare at Ashu.

Tawai squeezes himself in between me and Danna. "Dance with me, Uido!" he says. After that, I get no chance to speak to Danna again. Everyone in the tribe wants to dance beside me for a while—even the elders, who often prefer to watch rather than join in.

When the celebration is finally over, Ashu and Danna walk toward the bachelor hut with the other ra-gumul boys and I return to ours with Tawai and my parents.

Tawai unrolls his mat next to mine. "Did Lah-ame teach you how to look into the future?" he asks.

"I can try to see ahead if I must," I reply. "But it is far better to wait for the messages the spirits send us."

"So can you tell if the strangers will be back?"

"Probably, now that Pulug-ame has calmed the waves again," I say. "Why? Are you worried about them?"

"I want to see Ragavan again." Tawai sighs. "I asked the elders about the strangers' world but none of them will tell me much."

I say nothing, wanting to end the conversation.

But he goes on. "I wish their island was closer so we could swim over and see how they live. I hope they come soon, now that the rainy season has ended."

It concerns me that Tawai's curiosity seems to have grown, like moss spreading across a damp rock. Then I remind myself that I, too, was curious about the strangers. And listening to the sweet sound of Tawai's breath, I fall asleep.

21

The next morning I hurry to Natalang's hut, hoping to go gathering with her. To my surprise, although I am early, she has already left for the jungle. I twist and untwist the bark strap of the empty gathering bag hanging from my shoulder, wondering unhappily if she and I will ever be friends again. Standing by myself inside the circle of round huts, I feel lonely.

But an instant later Danna walks up and takes my hand. His palm is dry, his grip strong. At his touch, my heartbeat quickens. I feel as though a hummingbird is fluttering inside my chest.

"I was waiting for you," he says. "Shall we go to the beach?"

"Should you not go hunting soon?" I ask.

"Yes, but we had hardly any time together last night. The tribe can do without food from me today. Come."

We arrive at the beach to find Tawai wading in the shallows, his bow drawn. But instead of looking down into the water for fish, I see he is gazing into the distance. Danna points at him and whispers, "Look at Tawai pretending to fish. He is probably hoping the strangers come again."

"Tawai," I call out. "Why do you keep staring out to sea?"

Tawai's back stiffens. "I am looking for fish, Uido," he says.

"Then why are you—" My words are cut short as Tawai's arrow pierces through the waves, scattering a group of fish. He snatches up the wriggling body of a *tarcal-ta*. Holding it tight, he pulls his arrow out from deep inside. Then he walks up the beach, puffing his cheeks out proudly. He tosses the fish on the sand, where it squirms at his feet, and says a quick prayer of thanks to Biliku-waye and Pulug-ame.

We gather around to honor the fish's spirit with a moment of quiet until it lies still.

Danna breaks the silence. "Well done. Tarcal-ta is the tastiest fish in the ocean."

Tawai looks pleased and runs down the sand again to catch a few more.

Danna holds me back. "Let us swim, Uido." He scoops me into his arms and runs away from Tawai.

"What are you doing, Danna? I am not a child." I giggle, sounding like Natalang. Lifting me higher, he dashes into the surf.

"Put me down," I say, although feeling Danna's arms around me makes me want to be held closer.

He drops me into the cold water. "Catch me if you can!" he shouts, plunging into the waves.

I swim through the breaking waves, but Danna is far ahead. I take a big breath and dive underwater to go faster.

I keep my feet together, hands at my sides, my body curving like a dolphin's. Patches of reef sparkle beneath me like flowers and different-colored fish swim among them like underwater butterflies.

I pull alongside Danna and lift my head above the ocean's surface. "You may be taller now," I say, "but I am a stronger swimmer."

Danna grins and reaches underwater for my hand. An anemone stuck to a rock beneath us waves its arms at him as though it, too, wants to touch his body. For a while, we float together. It feels wonderful to drift like seaweed, aimless and lazy. Carried by the ocean, my body and spirit feel lighter.

"Shall we race back?" Danna asks.

We turn back to shore, my long strokes carrying me slightly ahead of Danna. But he pulls in front of me the instant our shadows ripple over the shallows, frightening a ray.

I try to catch up with Danna but cannot. In no time, he stands in the ankle-deep water near the shore, laughing at me. "Faster!" he calls.

He strides out of the waves, his wet skin dazzling against the white sand. I slow down to gaze at the water trickling across the scars decorating his arms and legs. A pleasant shiver creeps up my back as I walk out of the surf toward him.

Just as our hands meet again, I hear Tawai shout, "*Olaye, olaye, odo-lay, odo-lay!* Ragavan is coming!"

22

Tawai is already halfway up a coconut tree near the southern end of the beach, where the strangers' boat is approaching. "You should climb this tree instead of standing on the beach all day," he shouts down to the boy who is on watch. "I can see everything from up here."

"Not everyone is a monkey like you," the boy replies, before alerting the tribe. "*Olaye, olaye, odo-lay, odo-lay!* Come, everyone! The strangers are here again."

I stare in shock at the metal boat approaching our reef. "Danna, do you think the spirits have forsaken me? Why did I have no dream about the strangers' arrival this time? Every other time, I knew before they came."

"Perhaps the spirits have other messages for you," Danna says. "They cannot always tell you everything, Uido. I am sure there is much Lah-ame does not see."

I know Danna is right. Still, I shift from one foot to the other, unsure of what to do and upset that the spirits did not warn me about Ragavan's approach.

"Do you want to leave?" Danna asks, as though he senses my unease.

"No. I would feel worse not seeing what the strangers do."

I hear the splash of paddles as Ragavan and his two men row ashore in their wooden canoe. They jump out and start piling coconuts and bananas on the sand. Ragavan has a yellow bag on his back that looks a little like our boar-skin water bags.

Suddenly, my little brother squeals like a frightened boar. To my horror, I see Tawai tumble out of the tree and onto the ground. His body hits the sand with a soft thump.

We rush up the beach to Tawai's side, fear carrying my legs ahead of Danna's. Bending over my little brother, I lay my palm down flat on his chest.

"Tawai!" I say. "Are you all right?" My hand trembles with anxiety until I feel the steady throb of his heart.

Tawai sits up and chuckles. "Did I scare you?"

I grab Tawai's head with both my hands, kiss his forehead, then give his ear a hard twist. He squeaks.

"You silly fool!" Danna says, hugging Tawai to his chest.

"I was so glad to see Ragavan again, I forgot to hold on tight," Tawai says. "But it is not a tall tree."

I look Tawai over closely. To my relief, he seems to have escaped with no more than a badly grazed knee.

"I am all right, Uido." He scowls. "I was halfway down before I fell off."

I reach for the medicine bag at my waist but Lah-ame's warning flashes into my mind. I hesitate with my hand on my pouch, unable to decide if cleaning Tawai's small cut would be wrong.

"Uido?" Danna asks. "Is something wrong?"

"Lah-ame said I must not try to heal anyone until I fight my spirit animal," I say.

"You must fight a spirit?" Danna sounds worried. "When? Why?"

"It is hard to explain." I do not want to frighten Danna by saying any more about the test ahead of me. I gaze at Tawai, who looks as well as he did earlier that morning. "Perhaps it is best if I use no medicines on his cuts."

"His leg does not seem badly hurt," Danna agrees.

As we discuss what to do, Ragavan approaches us wearing a half-smile that stretches his lips but does not brighten his face. He feels Tawai's wrist, shakes his head and forces Tawai to lie back down.

"Leave Tawai alone," I say angrily to Ragavan, though I know he cannot speak our language.

Ignoring me, Ragavan slides the yellow bag off his shoulder. He opens the bag with a sound like the buzz of a mosquito and pulls out a large white box with two crossed red lines on top. Ragavan takes a see-through vessel out of the box. He opens it and the stench of the medicinal juice inside wakes me from my moment of curiosity.

I lunge toward Ragavan to pluck the vessel out of his hands. Danna tries to help by catching hold of Ragavan's arms. But it is too late.

Tawai grabs the vessel and pours some juice onto his leg. He shrieks.

"I told you not to use it," I say, terrified the juice has hurt him.

Tawai stops making faces and says, "This medicine makes my skin prickle. It feels funny. Not like Lah-ame's."

I hear footsteps pounding down the sand. Several hunters come out of the jungle with their bows drawn, among them Ashu and his two friends.

"We heard you scream," Ashu says. "What happened?"

Tawai speaks excitedly about Ragavan's medicine.

Ashu puts his arrows back into his quiver. "I thought you were supposed to be the one to cure people, Uido," he says with a smirk.

Feeling hurt, I do nothing but watch as Ragavan pinches the skin from Tawai's open cut together and covers it with a flat, pinkish brown strip.

"Look!" Tawai points at his leg. "Ragavan stuck my cut back together!"

The hunters gather around us, along with some ragumul girls who have just arrived. Ashu and his friends tell them how Ragavan helped Tawai with his powerful medicines.

Meanwhile, Ragavan reaches into his bag and takes out another box, this one only about as long as his thumb. Kneeling in front of Ashu, he holds it out as if he wants Ashu to take it.

Ashu tries to open the box, but the lid seems to be stuck. He tosses it on the ground in disgust.

"Open the box, Ragavan," Tawai says. "Show us how."

Ragavan smiles as though he understands. His hairy

fingers push at the side of the box and slide it open. Inside are tiny wooden twigs—all perfectly straight, all the same size. Each stick has a tiny red berry at the very tip, but they are too straight to be anything that fell off a tree.

Ragavan stands up and holds the box well above anyone's reach. With one quick movement, he strikes the red part of one twig against the side of the lid. At once, the twig bursts into a small flame.

We all step back. Some people cry out in fear. Others seem shocked into silence. Never before have we seen fire kindled so quickly, without any ceremony. Ragavan does not say anything in his own language to thank the spirits for the gift of fire. Worse, he blows out the flame and throws the twig carelessly away.

"Look how fast Ragavan lights a fire!" Tawai says, hopping up and down like a tree frog. "What a clever man!"

But Ashu's lips curl in a sneer. "I, too, can make fire from this twig!" he says to Tawai. He opens Ragavan's bag wide and we see it is stuffed full with boxes of magic fire twigs just like the one Ragavan is holding. I hear a hunter whisper in awe, "He has hundreds of boxes!"

I expect Ragavan to take the bag back from Ashu, but instead Ragavan grins. He looks pleased rather than upset by Ashu's rudeness.

Ashu takes a stick out carefully, rubs it against the side of the lid like Ragavan, and watches as it bursts into flame. My people back away still farther, but their eyes are on Ashu.

"Fire is sacred," I hiss at my brother. "You should know better than to play with it."

Ashu's nose flares in anger. "Stop telling me what to do, Uido."

"I want a magic twig," Tawai begs Ragavan. "Please?"

Ragavan pats Tawai's head and gives him a whole box. My little brother takes it with a joyful smile.

"No, Tawai," I say.

Danna snatches the box out of my little brother's hands and gives it to me. I crush it angrily in my fist.

"Give it back!" Tawai says. But then Ragavan pours the rest of the boxes from his bag onto the sand. Tawai grabs a box and skips away from me and Danna. Ragavan waves his hand at Tawai as if to say farewell and walks down the beach to join his friends, who wait near their canoe.

The crowd on the beach thickens. In the distance, I hear the steadily fading drone of the strangers' boat leaving our island.

I search for Kara, wishing he were here to help me control my brothers. But he must be deep in the jungle hunting. The others around us seem both amazed and scared by the fire twigs. One of my uncles murmurs prayers under his breath as he rubs his bone necklace between his fingers. I see a child reach for a box of twigs but his mother pulls him back.

"Natalang!" Ashu calls out, lighting another flame. "Do you want to try this?"

I notice then that Natalang is coming down the beach,

digging stick in hand, her bark bag swinging as she walks. She smiles at him, her eyes wide with admiration.

A few other ra-gumul girls and women are with her, Mimi among them. Mimi pushes through the crowd and asks, "What is happening here, Uido?"

Tawai answers, "Ragavan gave us a wonderful gift! I can make fire. Watch." He tries to set a magic twig on fire, but the flame jumps up and licks his thumb. He squeals, drops the stick and sucks his finger.

Mimi strikes his hand down, trembling with horror. But even our mother's presence does not stop Ashu. "Here, little brother, watch this," Ashu says, lighting another twig.

I storm up to Ashu. "Stop."

"Ragavan is more powerful than you will ever be, Uido," Ashu says. "Not only does he heal better than you do, he also knows how to capture fire. We have new magic. We have fire twigs."

"We have new magic! We have fire twigs!" Tawai begins to chant.

He is cut off by a woman's cry. "Lah-ame is here!"

23

The crowd parts to let Lah-ame through. He looks as close to rage as I have ever seen him. Lah-ame has never punished anyone before, but sensing his anger, I fear what he might do to the boys.

I move to Tawai's side and slap my hands over his mouth. "Be quiet, Tawai, please."

Lah-ame grips Ashu's chin and turns my brother's face up. "Look at me," he commands. He blows his breath across Ashu's cheeks, but his breath is fierce as a storm wind. Ashu's eyes roll from side to side, unable to hold Lah-ame's gaze.

"Have you anything to say, Ashu?" Lah-ame asks.

I see Ashu's mouth open slightly but he makes no sound.

Lah-ame's hands move down Ashu's neck and squeeze tight. For an instant, Lah-ame's fingernails appear to me like an eagle's talons, ready to pierce Ashu's skin and rip him apart. But all Lah-ame does is pull Ashu's necklace up over his head.

"A boy who is so disrespectful of his ancestors' ways does not deserve to wear their bones around his neck,"

Lah-ame thunders. As the tribe watches in shock, Lah-ame starts snapping the bones of Ashu's chauga-ta in half. Inside my mind, I hear a terrible scream—as though the spirits of our ancestors are crying because of Ashu.

Something inside Ashu seems to break at the sound of the bones cracking. His shoulders fold inward and I see him hunch forward, hugging his chest tightly, as though it hurts.

Lah-ame flings the broken necklace at my brother. "I return your chauga-ta with four bones broken. If you ever dare behave this way again, I will throw it into the ocean, along with your bows and spears and arrows."

Ashu catches his chauga-ta with shaking fingers. "I am sorry, Lah-ame," he murmurs.

"Louder," Lah-ame says. "What for?"

Ashu's head drops to his chest. "For dishonoring the spirits of our ancestors."

"Now, break the strangers' fire twigs and throw them into the waves."

Without even glancing in my direction, Lah-ame walks away. All around me, I hear sighs of relief, like a wind blowing through the leaves of a great tree. The crowd breaks up into little groups and most people start wandering back into the jungle or the village, but I stay on the beach with Mimi and my brothers, worried that Lah-ame is angry with me too, for not preventing my brothers from using the fire twigs.

Ashu and his friends collect the boxes of sticks and throw them into the water as Lah-ame commanded. After they are done, Mimi pulls Ashu toward me and places our hands against one another, forcing our palms to touch. "No more argument, children," she says.

Ashu grunts something, but his eyes refuse to meet mine.

I struggle to find words of peacemaking. "When we were children, our quarrels washed away as quickly as footprints on the beach. Can we not let that happen again?"

"Go away," he mutters and stalks off down the beach.

Mimi strokes my cheek. "I am sorry, Uido. Your brother has an angry spirit."

Tawai approaches Mimi. "I caught a tarcal-ta this morning. Do you want to see it?" Already he seems to have forgotten what just happened. Mimi gives me a hug and follows Tawai to his fish.

I look around the beach, hoping Danna is waiting for me. But before I spot him anywhere, I overhear Natalang telling one of her sisters, "I know it was wrong, but is Ashu not brave? He is the only one who was not afraid of the strangers' magic!"

Her words feel like thorns piercing my ear. Hurt by her and Tawai and Ashu, I run as fast as I can, away from them, away from our village, away from the tribe and into the jungle.

24

I go deeper and deeper into the jungle. Confused thoughts whirl like storm clouds in my head. How quickly I agreed to become Lah-ame's apprentice, not knowing the training would push Tawai and Natalang so far away. The spirits seem to have forsaken me too—forgetting to send a warning dream before the strangers' arrival this morning. Even Lah-ame ignored me just now. But I am not sure what more I should have done to control my brothers' behavior.

I hear footsteps close behind and glance back to see Danna's stocky frame gaining on mine. "Uido!" he calls out. "Is something wrong?"

We sit together on a fallen tree trunk. I lean my head against his shoulder.

"Sometimes I wish I had never started the training. How will I ever lead our people if I cannot even be friends with my own brother?"

Danna encircles my waist with an arm. His touch is calming. "Ashu and his friends left the beach saying they were going hunting and would not be back for a few days.

I think they are too ashamed to face the tribe—at least for the moment."

"But Danna, Ashu will be back sooner or later. And so long as he is part of the tribe, he will always fight me."

"Many En-ge want to see you become oko-jumu, Uido. I am not the only one who supports you."

I sigh. "Sometimes I am not sure I will ever be able to protect the tribe from the strangers as well as Lah-ame does. To tell the truth, I am curious about Ragavan's ways myself. If it was not for that, maybe I would have acted faster today."

"Even Lah-ame must have had trouble keeping the tribe safe when he was young," Danna says. "I am sure the elders remember his early mistakes. And anyway, I sense a change in you already. Your body looks as strong as a leader's."

"Did you like the old Uido better, Danna?"

"I like Uido," he says simply, placing my hand on his chest. The steady thud of his heart soothes me. "Your spirit may travel too fast for me to keep up, but I will always be here, waiting, every time you return from the Otherworld."

In the sunlight that drizzles like honey onto Danna's shoulders, he looks more beautiful than ever. We bend toward one another. My lips wander across his smooth cheeks and chin. We kiss once, twice, four times.

After a while, Danna breaks away, murmuring, "I found a new beehive. Shall we collect some honey?"

"But we have not been chewing the *tonh-je* leaves," I say. "The bees will sting me. Would you like me better with a swollen face?"

"I would never let anything bite you. I have tonh-je leaves." He reaches into the bag that hangs from his quiver, pulls out a few tonh-je leaves, starts chewing on one and pushes a few into my mouth. I crush a handful of leaves and smear them over him. With the tips of his fingers, he works the tonh-je juice into my skin. His touch feels as soft as the stroke of a butterfly's wings.

"Why are you trembling?" Danna asks. "What is wrong now?"

"It is just—our friendship is changing. Lah-ame says to an oko-jumu the tribe must always come first. I think that is why he never took a woman. But I cannot imagine being alone and spending every rainy season away from the tribe like he does."

"Imagine being married, then, like the women oko-jumu before you." Danna turns my face to his and blows gently across it. His breath, thick with the tonh-je scent, makes me feel light-headed and my concerns seem to drip away like honey from a comb.

Danna pulls me to my feet and we walk to the bee colony.

"Look." Danna points at a beehive that hangs halfway up the tree. "Wait here while I get it?"

"I climb as well as you," I tell him.

He grins. "All right. Ready?"

With the help of the thick vine encircling its trunk, we pull ourselves up. Our hands press against the bark and our toes find footholds in the rough trunk. Soon we are near the hive.

We blow into the air. The bees scent the tonh-je and grow drowsy. They settle on our bodies, droning *mmbbzzz, mmbbzzz*. Far below us, in the midday light, the jungle floor is mottled with shadows like a moth's wing.

"Biliku-waye, Pulug-ame, spirits of the Otherworld, thank you for showing us this food." Danna works until the comb comes away in his hands. We scramble down.

"I have never plucked a hive so easily. Not stung once." Danna pierces the comb. With a sticky forefinger, he teases my lips apart. I lick his finger, then let my tongue slide down its honey-sweet length. Cool air rushes into my throat and tickles me. I break off a tiny piece of comb and hold it to his mouth. He nibbles the edge and slurps at the thick liquid that dribbles out.

We break off other bits of the comb, suck them dry and spit out the wax. But we save most of it to share with the others. While we linger beneath the tree, the sky darkens as though it were evening instead of just past midday. A sudden downpour begins. I stare at the lightning Biliku-waye draws overhead by scratching lines in the sky with her pearl shell.

"What does Biliku-waye say?" Danna asks.

Thunder breaks and I wait for my spirit to sense an image after the next flash of light, just the way Lah-ame taught me. As the lines of white tear apart the gray clouds above, I see a picture of evil white spirits reaching out to capture one of us with their skeleton-thin fingers.

"Illness," I whisper, shuddering. "The lau are searching to catch someone's spirit."

Thunder booms again, like a drum beating out an alarm. We race back to the village.

25

The rain stops as we enter the clearing. But not one happy face greets us.

People are clustered in front of Lah-ame's hut: elders, children, a few men, and all the women. Nobody says a word as Danna and I push through to the center of the group. There, I see Lah-ame kneeling on the ground, bending over Tawai.

My little brother's eyelids are half closed. He shivers feverishly. My parents sit beside him, leaning against one another.

I drop the honeycomb and rush to Lah-ame's side. He strokes Tawai's body with an eagle feather—trying to find the lau that has captured my brother's spirit.

I crouch down beside Lah-ame. "What is wrong with my brother?"

"The strangers carried a disease spirit to our island. It has leaped into Tawai and made him ill." Lah-ame shakes his head.

"How can I help?"

"We need a cooling paste," he says.

I enter Lah-ame's hut, my mind so full of worry that

for an instant I cannot remember how to make the medicine. But then I find his store of heartseed vine. Praying to the plant's spirit to help Tawai recover soon, I grind the leaves into a paste and rush outside again.

Lah-ame dips his hand into the paste and spreads it on my brother's forehead. I see Tawai's temples throbbing. "Go, lau, go. Go out of this body," Lah-ame chants.

But the lau does not answer his call. Tawai groans, "My body hurts."

"Uido, bring a drink to cure pain," Lah-ame says. I return to his hut, where I squeeze coral berries into a juice to soothe body ache. Lah-ame pours it down Tawai's throat.

But Tawai's body will not take the medicine. A few moments after it passes his lips, we watch him vomit it back out.

Lah-ame looks up at the crowd. "Let all leave but Tawai's family," he says. "The lau inside him is a greedy one. It may catch anyone who comes too near."

An anxious murmur spreads through the crowd and slowly people begin to leave.

Danna lingers at my side. "I will stay with you," he says.

"No," I whisper to Danna, thinking I could not bear it if the lau caught his spirit too. He takes my hand, but I pull away. "Lah-ame knows best," I tell him. "Do what he says, Danna, please."

"Shall I look for Ashu?" Danna asks. "He only left this morning. He cannot be that far away yet."

"Tawai will get better before Ashu returns from his

hunt. There is no need for Ashu to hurry back." I speak with a confidence I do not feel.

Danna lets my hand drop. He blows gently on my cheeks and walks away.

Kara carries Tawai into Lah-ame's hut and I follow. He lays Tawai down on a reed mat and then sits beside Mimi.

Throughout the rest of that long day, Tawai worsens. He coughs up everything except fresh water from Lah-ame's nautilus shell vessel. As evening approaches, he no longer tries to speak, and his silence frightens me more than hearing him moan. He does not respond even to Mimi's touch. Though his body is burning hot, he shivers like a spiderweb caught in a storm.

Only once before has Lah-ame failed to heal—eight seasons ago, when one of Kara's sister's babies fell ill. Now, Tawai's eyes remain closed, like my little cousin's did before she died. After her death, Mimi said babies' spirits were the hardest to keep alive because they were like tiny plants just climbing out of the earth. But the older a spirit grows, the sturdier its roots, and the firmer its grasp on this world.

I tell myself Tawai's body is halfway grown. It will struggle hard to hold on to his spirit. "Biliku-waye, Pulug-ame, spirits of the Otherworld and of my ancestors, let my brother become well," I plead softly.

Lah-ame leads us outside, where I see the purple bruise of dusk spreading across the sky. "I cannot sense Tawai's spirit," he says. "It has wandered too far away to hear my call."

"How can that be?" Mimi asks.

"His spirit wants to be cured by the strangers' medicine," Lah-ame replies. "They carried this lau to him. Tawai will not be healed by me."

"Why?" Mimi says. "Why can you not cure him?"

Lah-ame runs a hand across his wrinkled forehead. "I have already told you. The lau has taken over Tawai's body. His own spirit has wandered far away."

"He is only a boy," Kara says. "A child. His spirit is trusting."

"Not in me." Lah-ame's voice is tired but firm. "His spirit wants to travel across the sea, not return to the heart of the jungle."

Kara looks hollow, like a dead tree trunk with its insides scraped out. Mimi clings to him like a withered vine. "You can save him, Uido," she whispers. "I have faith in you." Then my parents return to our hut.

Lah-ame hugs me for a moment and lets go. "I have tried everything we know again and again, Uido. There is nothing more I can do for Tawai. I am sorry."

Leaving me alone in the clearing, he walks away into the jungle. But as long as Tawai is still alive, I cannot walk away as Lah-ame has done.

In the life of the jungle, the death of one small boy means little. Every day the spirits watch the deaths of countless beings. But Tawai has a special place in my life. A place I want to hold on to.

Surely there is a chance that Tawai will respond to my call. My healing touch may not be as powerful as Lah-ame's, but I am Tawai's sister. His spirit has been close to mine all our lives.

As I return to Lah-ame's hut, his warning echoes in my mind again about trying to heal before meeting my spirit animal. Ignoring it, I close my eyes and move my hands over my little brother's body, searching for the lau. But Lah-ame is right—I cannot feel where the illness is lodged inside. All I sense is a pale cloud spreading across his body.

My hands tremble as I place them on Tawai's chest. Using the beat of his heart as my guiding rhythm, I send my spirit out to search for Tawai's. My spirit leaves Lah-ame's hut and floats across the clearing.

For a moment, I think I see a faint shape swinging on the vine hanging behind the bachelor hut, where Tawai loved to play when he was younger. But it disappears as I come closer.

I drift to the beach where Tawai fished so often and gaze out across the ocean in the direction the strangers come from. There, in the distance, I see the glow of a spirit moving away over the waves, farther and farther from our island's shores.

"Tawai!" I call. "Come back. Come to me." But he has slipped beyond my reach.

My spirit returns alone to Lah-ame's hut.

I slump against the curved wall. As Lah-ame said, Tawai's spirit has left us and gone in search of the strangers' island, because it wants to be cured by them.

In the loneliness of the hut, I try to think of how an

oko-jumu should heal a boy whose spirit has more faith in strangers' medicines than in our own.

Perhaps I should follow Tawai's spirit across the water and take his body to the strangers' world. There must be at least a chance that the strangers and I could work together on their island to coax Tawai's spirit back into his body. But if I cross over to the strangers' world, my tribe may think Ragavan's medicines are better than ours and lose faith in me and in the En-ge ways.

A soft groan escapes Tawai's lips. The sound cuts into me like a knife. Maybe I have walked the spirit paths for nothing. But I am not yet oko-jumu.

Tonight I am only a girl who cannot watch her little brother die.

III

ACROSS A STRIP OF SEA

26

Tawai's body is hot to my touch. He moans as I struggle to hoist him onto my shoulders, no longer the baby brother I once carried with ease.

I make my way to the beach and head straight for our canoes. I set Tawai's body inside the smallest one and drag the canoe toward the ocean. Praying for Biliku-waye's understanding and protection, I shove the canoe into the surf and jump in.

Branches of coral reach out like sharp fingernails, threatening to scratch holes into the boat. I give all my attention to getting past the reef. Soon the waves toss us into deeper water. Although I have never canoed on an open sea full of crashing waves, this skill feels surprisingly natural to me. My spirit seems to guide the movement of my arms and help me stay afloat.

I try to remember all Lah-ame taught me about the wind and the current and how to set a course by the stars. Praying to my ancestors to guide me across the ocean they traveled long ago, I row forward. Chants from the early days of our tribe enter my mind. I hear the words Lah-ame sang about the time when all the islands belonged to people like us. The memory of this watery path ahead has been tattooed into my spirit. Glancing over my shoulder, I see that we are already farther from my island than I imagined.

Then, through the darkness ahead, I hear a voice. Its tone is commanding.

Go back.

Clutching my oar, I keep rowing.

Clouds hide the stars above, darkening the night. The waves around us grow taller.

Return to your island.

Lightning tears across the sky and a sudden thunderstorm breaks. But despite the howling rain and the roaring sea, I guide the canoe onward. It is not for nothing that I walked the spirit paths.

The rain makes my eyes sting, but I force them wide open. In the next flash of lightning, I glimpse something monstrous writhing in the water. For a moment I think I have lost my mind. Then I see it again.

A pale creature is rising up out of the water. It looks like a gigantic sea snake. With all my strength I try to move away from it. But like an unseen hand, the current pulls us toward the creature.

Lightning rips overhead again and I see that what I mistook for a sea snake is just one of eight tentacles of the most terrifying animal in the ocean—a giant squid. On our beach I have seen carcasses of full-grown whales strangled to death by these squid, patches of flesh torn off their bodies.

This squid's arms look ten times as long as our canoe. And they are slithering across the waves, coming nearer and nearer to our canoe.

Do not go to the strangers' island.

No matter how hard I row, the boat swirls closer to the squid.

I see a slimy tentacle touch the side of the boat. At once, it feels as if the monstrous creature is tugging my spirit out of my body, tearing my spirit away from me so that it could never return.

27

Lightning streaks overhead and I see two tentacles reach for Tawai. The nose of the canoe begins to dip.

"No," I scream. "Leave him alone. You came for me." Lunging sideways, I reach down into the water with my paddle and the canoe rights itself again.

Are you willing to endanger your entire tribe for the sake of one life?

"I am a healer," I reply. "Is it not my duty to do anything possible to save all my people? Especially my little brother?"

The voice is silent. But I feel the squid's tentacles still trying to rip my spirit out of my body. I have to concentrate with all my strength of mind while I fight to keep our boat from tipping into the ocean.

A wave throws me against the side of the canoe. My hands scrape against the wood. Blood thick as honey runs down my fingers and I taste blood in my mouth.

"I will protect every life in my care," I cry. Holding tightly to my oar, I paddle harder.

The direction of the current shifts. I feel it pushing us

along, helping me. Somehow we have broken free of the whirlpool.

The wind stops howling and the rain softens. When I feel the tentacles let go, I slap my paddle against the water in triumph. The squid's arms curl away from the boat. But as the creature starts to sink beneath the waves, I realize that its eight-armed body is a watery reflection of Biliku-waye's form.

Lah-ame's words echo through my mind. "I sense yours is a water spirit."

And I understand. This squid is my spirit animal, my guiding voice. If it disappears into the ocean depths forever, I will lose a part of myself.

"Wait," I call out. "Do not go!"

The creature does not seem to hear me. It slips farther underwater. The waves grow calm.

"Share your wisdom with me," I say. "Help me care for my brother and for my tribe."

The tips of a few tentacles are all that remain above the water now. I feel the creature's spirit moving farther away from me. I paddle forward as fast as possible, until I am close enough to touch it.

"We have both won," I whisper. Reaching into the water, I pull our two spirits closer together.

We are one.

I feel first my arms, then my forehead, plunging into the cold ocean. Salty water fills my nose and trickles into my ears.

The darkness around me feels soft, not frightening. It is as though I was never whole until just now, as though all my life I was seeking this other part of myself without knowing it.

I breathe underwater. The ocean waits to show me its secrets. Through my spirit animal's great eyes, I can explore the wonders hidden in the great depths. But I cannot swim away with her tonight.

In the world above the water, my brother still needs me. And so I return to myself and to Tawai. "Lah-ame has a friend among the strangers," I say. "Can you sense where this friend is? Would you help take my brother to him?"

The strength of this body is yours.

Looking up, I see the sky is clear of storm clouds. I turn the canoe toward the strangers' island again and paddle forward. My spirit animal's body dips beneath the waves. The current strengthens and I feel she is helping to pull us along.

I row throughout the night. In the first pale glow of dawn, I see a stretch of beach curved like a bow and lights sparkling farther inland. For once, I am glad to see signs of the strangers' world.

"Thank you," I say. "From here I must go on alone."

Her tentacles let go of the canoe.

Travel safely through the strangers' world.

The creature lingers near us for a short moment. Then she slips beneath the waves.

I paddle nearer to the shore. A rush of surf fills my ears as tall breakers lift the front of the canoe. The canoe tilts sharply and we slide into the water. I grab onto Tawai and barely avoid being hit by the boat as it rolls upside down above us.

Struggling to hold Tawai's head above the water, I swim as hard as I can for the shore, hoping it is not too late to save him. Waves foam around my shoulders. I keep my eyes on the light twinkling through the coconut trees. It beckons me closer and closer, encouraging my tired limbs to pull us through the surf until at last the water is shallow enough to stand in.

I crawl out of the sea and up the beach, half dragging Tawai's limp body. I feel my strength draining out of me.

In a desperate effort, I shout as loudly as I can, "Help! We are Lah-ame's people! Help us!"

For one last instant, I call to Lah-ame's friend with my spirit. Then everything swims in front of my eyes. My body drops onto the sand like the washed-up carcass of a squid.

28

The first thing I see when I open my eyes again is a flat gray smoothness overhead—like the roof of a cave, not the rough brown slope of a thatched En-ge hut. Not a drop of sunshine falls through.

I lie on a raised platform. Beneath me is a mat made of something softer than moss and whiter than the sand on our beach. Another mat, woven just as finely, covers my chest and legs.

But Tawai is nowhere in sight, nor are any strangers.

"Help!" I scream. "Tawai! Where are you?"

Just then, a part of the gray wall opens. Two people enter, their bodies covered in white, their hair straight and black. The man is brown-skinned like Ragavan, but the woman has yellowish brown skin and thick-lidded eyes, like my image of Lah-ame's friend.

"I am friend," the woman says slowly in the En-ge tongue. "Do not be afraid."

For an instant I stare at her in disbelief, wondering if this stranger really spoke our language.

"My uncle teaches me to talk En-ge," she says. "He is Lah-ame's friend."

Although the woman pauses between words, she speaks clearly enough that I can understand her. Hearing her talk about Lah-ame in our language makes me feel safer.

"Where is my brother?" I ask.

"Boy is alive. Do not be afraid. I am healer. I help your brother."

"You—you heal?" I stutter with excitement. "Are you an oko-jumu?"

"I heal," she repeats. "My name is Maya. Your name?"

"My name is Uido," I say.

"Ooo-eee-doh," she repeats slowly, like a child, making sure she is saying it correctly. Yet she is no child but a living woman oko-jumu. A wave of admiration leaps inside me. I want to ask her what her training was like, if it is harder for her to lead her tribe because she is a woman.

But those questions can wait. First, I need to make sure Tawai is all right.

"How is Tawai—my brother?" I say.

"Safe," Maya replies. "We are in healing hut. Early morning today my uncle hears you calling for help. He runs to beach and sees you and your brother there. He brings you both here, so I can help."

"My spirit called to your uncle's and he heard me. Thank you for helping us." I take one of her hands in both of mine and blow my breath across it. "Now, will you take me to Tawai?"

I jump off the platform and onto the cold floor. The walls begin to spin around me. I force myself to fight the dizziness, afraid that if Maya thinks I am not strong enough to stand yet she might not let me see Tawai.

"Eat first." Maya talks in her own language to the man, who seems to be her helper. He leaves and returns holding a basket filled with bananas as green as the ones we enjoy on our island. As soon as I bite into the firm flesh of a banana, I feel less exhausted.

Maya teaches me some words in her language: "room" and "door" and "window" and "chair" and "table," pointing around us while I eat. My head swims with the newness of everything around me. Even the Otherworld is more like our own than this one.

When I am done eating, Maya helps me into a "dress" made of "cloth." Finally, she leads me out of the room. I follow her and her helper into a similar room close by.

There, at last, I see Tawai.

29

My little brother lies on a sleeping platform. One of his bony arms is pierced by a thorn stuck to a hollow rope that is tied to a shiny pole. Seeing him there, alive, I feel a rush of happiness. But as I run to his platform, my chest fills with worry again, because he still looks unwell.

Sitting beside him, I bend down to rest my cheek against his forehead. His skin no longer feels burning hot and his breath sounds normal.

"Tawai?" I call out softly. I take his small hand in my palm, but he responds neither to my words nor to my touch.

"Uido," Maya says, "your brother is alive but not well. I try to heal your brother every way I know. Understand?"

"Maya, you have cured his body without finding his spirit. How?"

"What?" Maya looks bewildered. "Spirit?"

I try to explain, but Maya shakes her head and gives up trying to understand. An awkward silence stretches between us. If this woman is really a healer, she should have sensed that Tawai's spirit has not re-entered his body. Maya seems to know nothing about the spirits. Yet despite that lack in her knowledge, looking at Tawai shows me that she can somehow heal the body.

But Tawai's spirit needs my help.

I stroke Tawai's forehead. Perhaps it should not surprise me that his spirit is still roaming. After all, the strangers' ways are different from ours.

I untie the rattle from my bone necklace. But when I start shaking it, Maya's helper comes up and grasps my arm. Placing his finger on his lips, he says, "Shhh."

Maya steps between us. "What are you doing?" she asks me.

"I am also a healer," I tell her. "You need my help."

Maya shakes her head. "Our ways are different."

"Yes," I agree. "But let me help in my way."

Maya stares at me. "I do not understand."

"I brought Tawai here thinking his spirit would be cured by your medicines. Somehow you have kept his body alive. I thank you for it. But his spirit is not inside him yet. Maybe his spirit will listen to me now that I have followed it to your island. I want to coax it back into his body."

"How you do this?" Maya asks.

"I will stand near Tawai, shake my rattle and call to his spirit."

Maya speaks to her helper. "All right," she says to me.

I stand at the head of Tawai's sleeping platform and close my eyes.

Then I move my hands over my little brother's body to search for the lau inside. Somehow, Maya has taken it out and the evil spirit is not inside Tawai any longer. But neither is his own.

"Come back," I say. "Return to me, little brother."

I look around Tawai's sleeping platform but see no glimmer of his spirit light hovering by it. Slowly I move around the room, searching for the glow, shaking my rattle and calling out to it. In the light pouring in through the window, I see a brighter shape. Sensing Tawai's spirit there, within reach, I want to rush toward it at once. But instead, I wait for it to approach me.

"The lau is gone," I say softly. "Now you must return to your body."

The light comes a little nearer. I sense it is weak because it has stayed outside his body for so long. But I force myself not to worry.

"Come." I stretch out my hand and coax it nearer. "I am Uido. You have known me all your life."

Tawai's spirit hovers above my hand. "Trust me," I whisper. "I can guide you back. I am a healer."

The light loops itself around my wrist like a glowing bracelet. Slowly I walk back to Tawai. The spirit lets me carry it along.

"Tawai," I say, standing beside his sleeping platform. "The strangers are healing your body. But your spirit and body must come together if you are to stay alive." I move my hand close to Tawai's ear. "It is not your time to leave us, little brother," I whisper, stroking Tawai's earlobe.

The glow of his spirit disappears into his body. "Tawai?" I reach for his hand.

Tawai's eyes open slowly.

"Uido?" His voice is frail as he slides his fingers through mine. His grip is weak, but his touch is warm with life.

I bury my nose in my little brother's thick mat of curls. His hair tickles me, making me half laugh, half sob with joy.

30

hank you," I whisper to all the spirits of the Otherworld. "Thank you for helping me save my brother's life."

When I finally look up at Maya, she says, "I am healer for long but I never before see anything like what you do."

Tawai's eyes open wider as he looks around the room. He speaks slowly. "Where are we?"

"Do you remember falling ill, Tawai?" I ask. "Lah-ame could not save you, so I brought you to the strangers' island. This is Maya, oko-jumu in the strangers' tribe. Her uncle is a friend of Lah-ame's and he taught her our language. She cured you."

"Your sister helps me," Maya says. "I keep your body alive. That is all. I cannot heal you without your sister's help. I need her. She heals you like magic."

"You are much prettier than your tribesman Ragavan," Tawai says.

"Ragavan?" Maya's eyebrows shoot up in surprise. "Ragavan comes to your island?" Maya says, as though she wants to be very certain she understands.

"He brought us very sweet bananas." Tawai yawns. "Can I have a banana?"

"Sleep," Maya says. "I give you banana later."

"Your nose is round and pretty," Tawai says. "Not as long as Ragavan's." Tawai wiggles his own nose and Maya's helper laughs.

"Tawai," I say firmly, "you need to rest, like Maya says, so you can get better soon."

"But I want to know—"

"I will answer all your questions later," I promise.

Tawai's eyelids droop. An instant later, he is asleep again.

Maya, her helper and I leave Tawai's room. Taking my hand, Maya leads me to another room where we sit on chairs. I feel awkward not sitting cross-legged on the firm earth.

Now that I know Tawai is better, my thoughts turn to Ragavan. "How do you know Ragavan?" I ask. "He looks different from you. He must belong to another tribe."

"In my tribe, not all people look same," Maya says. "My tribe has many people with different color skin and eyes. Ragavan is my tribe. But he is bad man."

"Do not worry," I tell her. "Tawai likes Ragavan, but I do not. He brought the disease spirit that made Tawai ill."

"I am sorry Tawai becomes ill after Ragavan comes to your island." Maya sounds upset. "Some illnesses that do not harm us very much cause great harm to your tribe. Many of my people do not know you can catch diseases from us that might kill you. But I think Ragavan does not care even if he understands this."

It pleases me that she seems to distrust Ragavan. "Why do you dislike him?" I ask.

"Ragavan wants much." She points at a tree outside a window. "My uncle says Ragavan wants trees."

"Trees?" I ask, unsure if I understand Maya correctly. "Why would you need trees? You use stone and metal to make everything. Only Ragavan's small boat was made of wood—and how many canoes could your tribe need?"

"We make many things from wood." Maya runs her fingers across the edge of my chair. "This is wood." Her eyebrows come together and she thinks for a while before she says, "Your wood is precious."

"But trees grow everywhere." I still do not understand at all. "A rare shell or beautiful feather is precious."

"My tribe is much much much much bigger than your tribe." Maya spreads her palms as wide apart as possible. "We need many things. Much land. Our island does not have much wood now because we cut trees. So your island wood is precious for us now."

"But if our wood is so precious, why did Ragavan not come to our island earlier? Why did he leave us alone all this while?"

"Ragavan comes to my island only now. For long time before, he lives in another place far away." She sighs. "My uncle helps my tribe make rule that we cannot come to your island. But Ragavan does not care about rules. And he is very strong."

"But you are the oko-jumu! You must be more powerful than he is."

"My tribe is very different," Maya says. "Ragavan is much stronger than me, than my uncle."

Although I can see now how different the strangers are, it is hard to imagine a tribe in which the oko-jumu is not respected as a guide. I give up trying to understand them. But even if the reason is unclear to me, it is good to know that Maya dislikes Ragavan too.

31

Over the next four days, Tawai grows stronger. Sometimes, while he sleeps, I follow Maya around. I do not learn how she makes her medicines or how she heals, but I enjoy watching her work. Speaking in her own language, Maya sounds commanding and sure—almost like Lah-ame. Best of all, Maya promises that as soon as Tawai is well, she will take us to her uncle's home and from there, back to our island.

On the fifth morning after our arrival, Tawai is already awake when I enter his room. Maya, too, is there.

"Your brother is well," Maya says. "We go to my uncle's hut now."

But Tawai pleads, "Do we have to leave today? Can we please stay and look at this island?"

"I am tired, Tawai," I say. "I want to go home."

He begs again. And again.

I feel as though there are two strong tides pulling me in opposite directions. If I give in to Tawai, I might feed his spirit's fascination with the strangers, making it harder for him to return to our island. Then again, if we see more of this world, perhaps it will satisfy him and he will be happy to go home and stay there.

Seeing Tawai's lower lip tremble as he starts to cry, I finally give in, unable to disappoint him when he finally seems his old self again.

"My brother is not ready to leave," I tell Maya. "If I forbid him today, perhaps he will be tempted to return later."

"Or he forgets about our island quicker if he does not see it before returning to yours," she argues.

I wipe the tears off Tawai's cheeks. "We will go for a short walk with Maya—so you can see a little more of this place. But only a very short walk."

Tawai cheers up at once, but Maya sucks in her plump cheeks, making her round face look almost long. "Not good, Uido," she says.

"I know you will keep us safe," I say to Maya. "That is why I agreed to my brother's wish."

"I try." Maya's tone sounds angry. "I can only help little. Better we go to my uncle's home soon."

We follow Maya out of the room and through the healing hut, walking and turning through many rooms until I feel dizzy. But my little brother delights in everything— the hard floors that tire my feet and make them wish for moist earth, the still air that makes me long for a sea breeze. Every time Maya stops to speak to people, Tawai pulls at her hand, wanting to know whatever she says, reaching for everything she touches.

I avoid looking at Maya, worried that maybe she is right about looking around for even a little while. But it is too late now to change my decision.

32

Outside, the touch of the breeze around my legs and arms feels wonderful. I wish I could take off the dress and let the wind stroke my entire body. The sky looks gray here, but still, it rests my eyes just to see the clouds blowing overhead.

I almost scream when something comes at us, rumbling like thunder. It looks like a box-shaped animal with two huge, bright eyes.

"What is that?" Tawai breaks away from us and runs toward it. I race after him, Maya at my heels. We pull him back just as the thing stops with a high-pitched squeal.

"We call it 'car,'" Maya says. "Careful. Must not go near car."

As the car continues past us, I see that it is a kind of land boat. A man is sitting inside it, and some sort of magic is making it move. It leaves behind a gray cloud with a bitter taste that makes my throat itch. But the car delights Tawai. "Everything is better on this island," he says. "You have so many magical things!"

At Tawai's words, Maya's body stiffens. She leads us along a hard black path. Strangers point at us and whisper to each other as we go by.

Near a small, flat-roofed hut by the side of the path, we see a little child drinking something orange out of a see-through pitcher.

"I want to taste that, Maya, please," Tawai says.

Maya nods, disappears inside the hut and returns holding a pitcher full of bubbling orange water.

Tawai takes a gulp and laughs. "It is cold, Uido! It tickles my throat. Here, have some."

The bubbly orange water makes my tongue tingle, but I find it too sweet for my taste.

We walk past a man who is shouting at the top of his voice from behind a mound of bananas. Next to him, I see a child weeping. Unlike the other strangers, the boy has only a small piece of cloth around his hips. He is so skinny I can make out the shape of the bones in his chest and shoulders.

He wails as if he is hungry, but he cannot be—food is plentiful on this island, and there is a pile of fruit just beside him. I wait for him to take a banana, but he does not. Hearing the child's pitiful whines, I lose my patience with the strangers' ways. Tired of wondering what is wrong with the child, I take a fruit from the pile and hand it to him. Immediately, he runs away, clutching the banana to his chest as though it is precious. I stare after him, confused.

The shouting man leaps out from behind the fruit pile and blocks our path. He grabs my arm. I try to struggle free. He thrusts his face close to mine.

"Uido!" Tawai runs at the man. But the man tightens his grip and shakes me so hard that my head snaps back and forth on my neck.

Maya steps between me and the man, speaking to him rapidly and pushing him backward. The man lets go and I rub the back of my neck. Maya drops flat, shining circles into his palm. The man's hand closes over them and he walks back to the mound of fruit without telling me he is sorry.

"What did you give the man?" I ask Maya. "Why did he let me go suddenly?"

"We call it money." She holds a circle out to me. I roll it in my palm. It is shiny, as though it is made from metal. I bite it gently to see how hard it is.

"What will the man do with this money?" I see no use for such a tiny piece of metal.

Maya searches for the word. "Trade," she says after a moment. "I give man money. Man gives us banana."

"Why would anyone trade for food? Even the children of our tribe know better than to be greedy about food. It is everyone's to share."

Maya looks at the ground and says, "Our island has much food. But we do not all have food. There is much money. But not everyone has money."

I think of the yellow hill of bananas Ragavan brought

for our tribe—people he does not even know. Yet here, on his own island, there are hungry people. And even Maya did not help the hungry child or seem to think it was wrong to hoard fruit. I cannot understand how any tribe can allow their children to go without food.

Ahead of us, I see a woman thinner than even the boy. Her back is hunched but her skin is as black as mine, her hair as tightly curled, her lips thick as Natalang's. I wonder if she belongs to one of our sister tribes from Lah-ame's stories, or even perhaps to the part of our tribe that Lah-ame left behind on this island.

I smile at her, but she does not speak to me. Instead, she pulls at the arm of a man walking past us. The cloth over her body is muddy. Her palms are outstretched and she wails. I sense she is begging for something.

The man shouts at her in his language and raises his hand over his head as though to beat her. The woman cowers like a frightened animal, then turns, whining to Maya. Maya reaches into her bag and gives her a shining circle of money.

Tawai runs ahead but I reach out to touch the woman's sunken cheek. Her skin feels as dry as a withered petal. Worse, I hardly sense her spirit at all. It seems weaker than even Tawai's was when he was ill, almost as though it has already left her body.

"Let me help you," I say softly. "Please, tell me what you need." But the woman backs away from me and limps off to the side of the path.

Maya lays her arm across my shoulders. "We cannot help this woman, Uido."

"But she looks like me. Is she from our tribe? Lah-ame said he left behind hundreds of others."

"She is from tribe like yours," Maya says softly. "But after they try to live here, they become small and weak. Most tribes who come out of jungle lose their way."

"Why?" I ask, although I sense the answer. I feel a lone-liness here on this island. A loneliness that is darker and colder than anything I have felt, even when I journeyed alone through the swamp. It seems to come from the way the strangers live. Their huts feel like empty boxes; yet they fill the air outside to bursting with harsh noises. They have learned to capture water and light; yet they push away the spirits that live within water and light and all other things.

"Uido," Maya says, "in jungle, your people's lives are part of something bigger. Here, their lives break into small pieces."

"Why did they not return to their jungles?"

"Men like Ragavan cut trees. Kill animals. Then my people build houses where jungle was. Not many islands like yours still left."

"So where do my people live now?"

"Your tribe is gone," she says.

"Gone where? Another island?"

Maya shakes her head. "All En ge are dead."

"Dead?" My body feels suddenly heavy. I sink down to

sit on the hot path, unable to move forward. I never knew those others in my tribe, but still, they were my people.

"You see now?" Maya sounds desperate. "Some of other tribes are still alive, just smaller than before. But even they lose much when they try to live just like us."

33

Maya pats my back but her touch does little to comfort me. I ache for the warmth of Danna's hand.

Upset at myself for avoiding until now the full meaning of Lah-ame's warning story, I walk toward Tawai. He has stopped not far from us, in front of a woman who has glittering necklaces and bracelets spread out before her.

"Look how long this necklace is, Uido." He snatches one up. "It would hang down to Mimi's navel."

I pry it from his fingers, saying, "It is time to go back now."

Tawai pouts until Maya tells him we will go to her uncle's home in a car. At once, Tawai cheers up. We follow Maya back to a place outside the healing hut where several rows of cars stand. Tawai shouts and stamps his feet. "We are going in a land boat!"

Maya walks up to a blue car and opens a door like in a room. She sits on a chair inside. Tawai jumps up beside her. I climb in and squeeze close to Tawai.

The land boat growls and we jerk forward. Tawai squeaks with excitement as the ground outside the window moves faster and faster. We race away from the village of tall box-shaped huts and past a treeless patch of land covered with tall grass.

Soon we enter a jungle. I hear the *kuk–kuk–kuk–kuk* of a woodpecker tattooing holes in an old trunk. The trees reaching up on either side of us make me feel safer than I have in a long while.

But as we continue on, I worry that our jungle is no longer as safe as it once was. Surely once everyone knows about Tawai's recovery, they will be more curious than ever to explore the strangers' world for themselves. Even if they accept me as oko-jumu, it will be hard for me to stop them because I left to come to the strangers' island myself. And after we leave our island, people like Ragavan could cut down our jungles so we would have nowhere to return.

Yet even now, looking at the brightness in Tawai's eyes as he gazes outside the car, the guilt I feel about bringing him to the strangers' world fades. Whatever happens to our tribe and our faith in the old ways, at least Tawai will be with us. Perhaps my choice was wrong—but I could not have chosen otherwise.

34

All day, as the car moves across the strangers' island, Tawai chatters with Maya, asking about the car and the other magical things the strangers use. Even though Maya often tells him she does not know enough words in our language to explain, he keeps asking questions. But I remain quiet, wondering if by saving my brother's life, I have started on a path that will lead my people to their end.

At dusk we reach the top of a small hill. The land boat stops moving. Tawai yawns but is still excited enough to leap out when Maya opens the door. I step out of the car.

Here, as on our island, the breeze carries the taste of salt and the whisper of the sea. My body relaxes as the scent of leaf-rich soil rises up from the jungle encircling the foot of the hill. Already I feel close to home.

"Come," Maya says. Spread out across the hill are several huts. They are thatched with sloping roofs like ours. We follow Maya into the nearest one. A gecko lizard hanging on the door clicks its tongue, as though it is glad to see us.

Inside, I see a man bent over a shiny vessel, stirring

something over a low fire. He straightens up as we enter. Immediately I recognize him as Lah-ame's friend.

"This hut smells of cooked fish," Tawai says.

For a moment I feel sorry for the man and I wonder if he prepares his own food and eats all alone most nights. But there is a strength about the way he stands that reminds me of Lah-ame. The man's face is like a weather-beaten rock into which the wind has carved deep lines. His hair hangs in gray strips down to his shoulders.

Maya gives him a quick hug and they exchange a few words in their tongue. Then he speaks to us in En-ge.

"Welcome, Uido. Welcome, Tawai," he says softly. "I am Uncle Paleva."

He motions to a table larger than the ones in the healing hut. Tawai sits on a chair, looking quite comfortable even though it wobbles.

"My friend Lah-ame is well?" he asks.

"Very well." I want to say more, tell him of the affection in Lah-ame's voice when he spoke to me about Uncle Paleva, about the vision in which I saw him on the cliff, but I sense there is no need.

My short answer seems to satisfy Uncle Paleva. "Our spirits feel strongly bound to one another's," he says. "We often visit one another in dreams." He puts steaming bowls of food in front of us. "Eat well," he says.

I take a bite out of a chunk of fish floating in the soup. Although the fish is not one we eat on our island, my tongue enjoys the taste.

After we finish our meal, Tawai rubs his belly. "That was good. Thank you," he says, his eyelids beginning to droop. He stretches himself out on the mud floor and falls asleep almost at once.

"This is room where we eat," Maya says. "Not sleep."

"It does not matter," Uncle Paleva says. "Let him sleep here tonight. They leave early tomorrow."

Uncle Paleva turns to me. "Uido, I am glad you are here. There is a story in me waiting to be told." Although he has been away from our island for so long, he speaks our language easily. It is wonderful to listen to his voice.

"I like stories," I say. "It is too bad Tawai sleeps. He likes them too."

"You can remember my story and tell it again," Uncle Paleva says. "I give it to you." No one except for Lah-ame has ever gifted me a story before. Yet this gift from a stranger I find easy to accept. My spirit feels as though we are from the same tribe and have known each other for many seasons.

"A long time ago, when I was young," Uncle Paleva begins in a singsong voice, "I lived across the seas in a place called Burma. There, I fell in love with a beautiful girl. Her eyes were large and brown, and I never thought she would look well upon me because my people, the Karens, did not have much.

"But she loved me and we were married. Then one day, the leaders of Burma started fighting with the Karens. So my wife and I sailed away, never to return.

"We landed on this island. Here we made our home. We had three children together, all sons, and they were good boys, with big brown eyes like hers."

Uncle Paleva's voice falls to a whisper. "But one day my wife fell very ill. We took her to the healing hut where you and your brother stayed. But our oko-jumu could not save her life.

"We all mourned the passing of her spirit into the Otherworld. But by then our sons were grown and had moved away. I tried to live alone in our hut, but I could not. I did not weep often, because my sadness was too deep for that—but I also forgot how to laugh.

"One night I walked to the beach and pushed my boat into the waves. I floated into the sea, lay down quietly in my boat and waited for it to turn over and throw me into the ocean. But somehow, it never happened."

Maya interrupts. "Your boat was too good, Uncle."

"Yes." Uncle Paleva's voice rises like a gentle tide. "Somehow my boat carried me safely onto a stretch of beach. I lay there, like a piece of driftwood, until Lahame found me—hurt and bleeding. He looked terrifying. I thought the bones around his neck were from a person he had eaten. And despite my wish to die, I did not want to end up as his meal."

I laugh.

Uncle Paleva joins in my laughter. "Yes, I was foolish. Instead of eating me, he healed the wounds of my body and spirit. Your tribe took me in, and from them I learned how to laugh again. I hunted and fished with your men and ate the food your women cooked. I sang my wife's favorite songs, hoping my voice would carry to wherever she was. On your island, I felt I was part of something larger. I understood that to the spirit, crossing over from life into death is only the beginning of a new adventure, a start and not an end.

"I wanted to stay with your people, but Lah-ame told me that I should return here and teach my people to respect yours. He feared that others of my world would tempt the ra-gumul boys and girls of your tribe away from your island by showing them our magic. And he wanted me to find and help the En-ge who had chosen not to follow him.

"I agreed to go, but coming back here was not easy. How could I convince my people that although I had traveled to your island, they should not disturb you?"

I whisper, "I shall have the same problem now with my tribe, Uncle Paleva."

He nods and continues. "To keep my promise to Lah-ame, I had to learn many new things. I had to gain the respect of everyone on my island and become a leader that people listened to. I left the Karen village and went to a place called college, where there were wise people who taught me a great deal.

"Then I built this village we are in, where I welcome tribes whose homes have been destroyed. Here, I also invite people like me. We try to learn from and also protect tribes like yours."

"Protect them from what?" I ask.

"We try to help tribes save their jungle homes—or find new ones if their homes are already gone. We work to protect the animals and plants of these islands too."

"But why do people of your world want anything from us?" I say. "Maya tried to tell me that Ragavan wants our wood, but I still do not understand. You have so much here."

"There are some men who are just greedy, Uido," Uncle Paleva replies. "Always, always they want more and what they have is never enough. There are also a few people who believe our way of life is better than yours. They think you would be happier living in our world."

"Did these people stop you from helping the En-ge whom Lah-ame left behind?"

"I almost gave up my work when I realized your people were all gone," Uncle Paleva says. "But I was able to help save other tribes just like yours, Uido."

"How?"

"When an oko-jumu dies without passing on his wisdom, or when people lose faith in their oko-jumu, a tribe is weakened. This happened with the En-ge. But when an oko-jumu was able to lead a tribe forward by finding the right balance between the ancient knowledge and the new, the peoples' spirits remained strong. And then I could help them find ways to live in our world without losing faith in theirs."

"That gives me hope, Uncle Paleva. If other tribes are able to survive in your world, all is not yet lost for us," I say.

Uncle Paleva smiles. "Sometimes you think a path has ended, only to find it has led to something new. Once, I washed up on your island, and Lah-ame found me. Five days ago, you came ashore on ours, and we found you. Just as the wisdom of your tribe helped me build another future for myself, I pray that your time in our world will help rather than harm you."

For a few moments, the three of us are quiet. Then Maya fetches me a sleeping mat and wishes me good dreams.

"May your spirit have happy visions of the future, Uido," Uncle Paleva says, touching the place in the wall that makes the light go out. After they leave, I curl up beside my brother and think of Uncle Paleva's words.

Maybe the path across the sea was a new beginning. After all, it was between the strangers' island and ours that my spirit animal found me and made me feel complete. Here, a woman oko-jumu became my friend and together we cured Tawai. My thoughts drift over all I have found on this journey that gives me confidence, a confidence I will carry back to Lah-ame and Danna and the rest of my people.

As I lie in the dark, the scent of moist earth floats into the hut. It reminds me of Danna's skin. My chest swells with longing and I wish he were close enough to touch. It is a while before I fall asleep.

35

The next morning we leave for home with Maya and Uncle Paleva, in his metal boat. As soon as the strangers' island is lost from sight, Tawai pulls off the ugly cloth covering his body. I do the same. After being forced to hide my body for so many days, my bare skin enjoys drinking in the warm sunshine.

The sky looks bright and clear, but a mist hangs over my spirit, a sadness I do not understand. Tawai is well and we will soon be in the green shadows of our jungle. So I should be happy. Lah-ame might be upset with me for leaving, but once I tell him I have won over my spirit animal, he will surely be pleased.

I try to turn my back on the feeling and look at the dolphins leaping in front of the boat. Running my tongue across my lips, I taste the spray that flies off their smooth bodies. But still my spirit does not feel their joy.

"If our tribe had a boat as fast as this one," Tawai says, "we would catch many more turtles, because we would not be so tired from paddling. Everything you have is stronger, like the medicines that cured me."

"No," Uncle Paleva says. "Some of our medicines come

from the same plants in your jungles that your oko-jumu use. You also have magic to heal the spirit that we have forgotten."

"Your healers may even know medicine plants we do not," Maya says.

But Tawai does not seem to hear. He chatters on about how much easier our lives would be if we could use the strangers' magic.

Uncle Paleva sighs. "Tawai will tell the others about our world," he warns me. "And they will want to leave. My friend Lah-ame will be unhappy."

"I will find a way to protect my tribe," I say.

"May Biliku-waye and Pulug-ame give you the power to keep your people safe," Uncle Paleva says. "The En-ge taught me the beauty of silence. I learned that all things have spirits and are part of one great family. In my heart I still carry your people's love and it keeps me from the emptiness that sometimes enters our lives."

"Do not worry, Uncle Paleva. I have gained knowledge and confidence from visiting your people." I open my medicine bag and take out the dried leaf of an insect-eating plant. "Do you know what this is?"

Uncle Paleva rolls the leaf between his fingers. "Yes, it grows in our world too."

"I risked my life to find this plant because Lah-ame said it held a message for me that would help me guide my people. Only now do I see that its message lies in its survival. This plant thrives in the swamp where few plants can grow because it eats insects, as an animal might. In all other ways it remains like a plant. You see, it changed its behavior a little to survive in a new world, but never gave up its true nature. Perhaps we, too, can survive any challenges the future brings us if we learn some of your ways without giving up all of our own."

Uncle Paleva breathes in the leaf's scent. "A symbol of hope," he says. "A spirit that found balance between the ways of plants and animals, while remaining true to its plant nature." He smiles thoughtfully.

For the rest of the journey we fall silent.

I hear Tawai telling Maya about his friends and our family and then asking about hers. She says she has many friends, even a boyfriend. She laughs when he asks if they will marry and have babies together one day—and I am pleased when she answers that yes, they will. From the tone of her voice, I sense that she never worries that marrying and staying close to her tribe will interfere with her duties as an oko-jumu.

I glance at Maya, thinking how different she looks from Lah-ame. In some ways, maybe she is more the kind of leader I will be than Lah-ame is. Because after all, though we come from different tribes, we are both women.

Soon the rocky cliffs at the northern end of our island rise out of the blue water, and as we come nearer still, I see the crescent-shaped beach reaching toward us like a welcoming arm.

Uncle Paleva stops the boat outside the coral reef and remains on it.

"Will you not come with us?" I ask, surprised.

He shakes his head. "When I left your island, Lah-ame and I agreed it would be best if I did not return, bringing reminders of my world with me, unless it was necessary. Your tribe does not need my interruption." Gazing at the island, he smiles wistfully. "We are old men. Soon enough, Lah-ame and I will meet again in the Otherworld. For now, it is enough that you carry my loving greetings to him."

"But you are both strong," I say. "There are many years of life ahead for you in this world."

Uncle Paleva blows his breath across my cheeks. "*Ngig kuk-l-ar-beringa*, Uido."

I hug him close and return his words of farewell. "May your heart be in a good place, too, Uncle Paleva."

Maya lowers a canoe into the water and Uncle Paleva helps the three of us climb in. We each take a paddle and row toward shore. In the dark shadows of the jungle along the sand's edge, I see the stocky outline of Danna's body. My spirit feels a leap of happiness—but something also feels wrong, because although he runs toward us, he does not shout with joy to welcome us home.

Tawai says, "We are back!" He thanks Maya, hops into the shallow water and splashes ahead of us.

The boat scrapes against the sand and I step out. "May your spirit be well until we meet again, Maya."

"Be well." Maya squeezes my hand and rows away.

Danna is waiting for us, arms outstretched, but his smile is not as broad as usual. And looking into his eyes, I see something is wrong.

"Where is everyone?" Tawai demands. "Why is nobody else here to welcome us?"

Danna's breath feels unsteady on my cheeks. "Lah-ame is waiting for you, Uido," he says. "He told where you had gone and promised us you would return safely, after Tawai was healed. But Lah-ame is unwell. His spirit will soon be crossing into the Otherworld."

IV
ISLAND'S END

36

My feet feel heavy as we make our way back to the village. It upsets me that I did not sense Lah-ame's death approaching.

In the clearing, I see people bunched together outside Lah-ame's hut. As they notice our arrival, I hear soft voices: "Uido and Tawai are back, just as Lah-ame predicted." Mimi clasps me and Tawai against her as though she will never let go. She runs her long fingers through our curls, her chest shuddering with sobs.

"Welcome back, Uido," Kara whispers. I am shocked to see my father's strong back bent like a bow. Gently, I pull away from Mimi. The rest of the tribe greets me with a few smiles and soft touches on my shoulder. Then I enter Lah-ame's hut alone.

Lah-ame is stretched out on a mat and he looks as frail as Tawai did when he was ill. I squat down beside him and grasp his hand tightly. Already it feels cold to my touch. Only his gaze is as piercing as ever. Seeing me, he smiles.

"Lah-ame"—my voice shakes—"you must not leave me."

He chuckles. "Is that an order? If so, I should leave at once. It is long since another told me what to do."

"Stay, please—," I choke. I want to share so much with him—the meeting with my spirit animal, how I helped cure Tawai, Maya's distrust of Ragavan, the story Uncle Paleva gave me. And once Lah-ame is gone, there will be no one to answer all the questions I still have about the Otherworld, about leading the tribe into the future.

Lah-ame strokes my hand. "You are the one to take the En-ge forward. A man's body is not made to hold two lives; that is a woman's privilege. Who better than a woman to teach the tribe how to hold two worlds together?"

Lah-ame's voice sounds so weak that it terrifies me. "Do not leave me all alone," I plead.

"Surely Danna will see to it you never feel too lonely." Lah-ame's chest rattles as he laughs. "And so will the sea creature whose spirit you won over. But above all, listen to the beat of your heart and let that show you the way."

Tears prick behind my eyes. I try to hold them back, but they roll out, blurring my image of Lah-ame's thin body. "But how do I keep our island safe—the way you did? Have I set the En-ge on the wrong path?"

Lah-ame sighs. "Dearest daughter, I can no longer guide. Even a pregnant woman does not share the dreams of the baby who sleeps within her. You must dream of what lies ahead and take the tribe with you."

He reaches up and pokes my chest, forcing me to straighten up. But even that effort seems to tire him and he falls back onto his mat. "Keep your back straight as a spear, Uido."

"I am sorry," I say. I want to tell him how confused I

feel about my actions, that I regret my mistakes. But I stay quiet, sensing that he wants to say more.

"Enough with sorry." Lah-ame's voice drops to a whisper. I bend low, my ear close to his lips. He takes long pauses between words. "You saved Tawai's life by carrying his body to his spirit, but you have not been blinded by the strangers' magic. Most other tribes lost faith after the strangers surrounded them. So they died empty and dispirited. One day, the En-ge will also have to mix with strangers. But if you keep our spirits alive, we will never die out."

His voice slurs. "Uido, you are the storyteller now. Make our story end differently."

With a last effort, Lah-ame presses my face against his. But though I listen, hoping for another precious word from him, he says no more—just blows his breath on my cheeks. Then he lies back on his mat and I sense his spirit leaving, like a cloud disappearing into the sky.

I stumble out of the hut into Danna's waiting arms. From somewhere far away, I hear the cry of a sea eagle.

37

Later, I go back into Lah-ame's hut to attend to his body. The other women follow me, and one by one they kneel beside him, beating their breasts with their hands and weeping until they are exhausted.

Even Natalang mourns his death. When she has no tears left, Natalang comes to stand beside me. Hesitantly, she touches my elbow. I lean against her soft body, my head sinking into her shoulder. We cling together for a while, my tears washing away the awkwardness between us.

After the women are done weeping, they all leave, except for Natalang and Mimi. I crouch beside Lah-ame and run my hand over his arm. His body is as still as a fallen tree.

"We must bind him soon," Mimi says.

"Yes." My voice sounds far away. "There must be a rope somewhere in this hut."

"I will find it," Natalang says.

"Should we make the mourning clay?" I ask.

Mimi points at two bowls near the doorway. "We prepared some this morning, as soon as Lah-ame told us his spirit would be crossing over."

Natalang and Mimi help me decorate Lah-ame's body

with stripes of clay. When we are finished, Mimi says, "He told us you were to be treated as his daughter." She and Natalang cover my forehead with the rest of the clay, to show that I am in mourning for him as a member of his family would be. Then Natalang brings me a bark rope.

My eyes pool with tears. Together, we bend Lah-ame's stiffening legs and push his head and arms close to his knees. We tie his limbs together and bundle his body into his sleeping mat.

"He looks ready to reenter the earth," Natalang says gently.

The three of us carry him to the center of the clearing and lay him down so the men can bid him farewell. I watch Kara kneel, pounding at his chest and tearing at his hair, by Lah-ame's body. Ashu cries with his fists tightly clenched, and it pains me that my brother is angry even at this time of grief. Danna sobs quietly but for longer than anyone else.

Next we bring the children forward. Starting with Tawai, down to the youngest toddler in the tribe, they each breathe gently on Lah-ame's face for the last time.

Natalang, Mimi and the rest of the women leave the village and return with armfuls of palm leaves. Tawai and the older children help tear each leaf in two and hang them across every doorway to signal to the spirits that we have lost a loved one. Meanwhile, under the laurel tree behind his hut, the men set to work putting together a wooden platform for his body to spend one final night. Of the women, I alone stay with Lah-ame for the remaining death ceremonies. Using a tolma crystal, I shave Lah-ame's head until it is as shiny as a newborn's.

At dusk, I watch Kara lay Lah-ame's body to rest atop the finished platform. The laurel tree's white flowers look brighter to me than usual, shining like stars against its dark leaves. One of the elders brings a firebrand and Kara and his hunters light small fires around it, preparing to guard Lah-ame's body overnight so that his spirit can return to bid his body a final farewell.

Mimi tries to force me to eat some of the evening meal, but my throat feels too tight to swallow much food. In the end, she gives up, telling me to rest in Lah-ame's hut. "All his things belong to you now," she says.

It feels strange to enter Lah-ame's hut knowing he is not there. "Lah-ame?" I whisper into the emptiness, wanting to sense his presence, willing his spirit to comfort mine. But he is gone now, too far away to answer.

I try to sleep but my head aches to rest against Danna's sturdy chest, feeling the steady thud of his heartbeat. I creep outside and see Danna standing still as a rock against the flickering light of the many flames around the platform. Silent with his own grief, he is watching the hunters who guard Lah-ame's body—and I feel it would be wrong to disturb him with my sadness.

Instead, I crawl into my family's hut and slide between Tawai and Mimi. But even the warmth of their bodies on either side does not soothe the ache in my chest.

At dawn, I awaken and leave the hut. Mist stretches between the earth and the sky, soft as a baby's hair. Through it, I can see the glow of the still-lit fires around Lah-ame's platform. I should tell the men their watch is over, but I do not want to bury his body yet. So I slip away to the beach. The sun rises, warming the sand, but I shiver with a cold sadness.

Sitting cross-legged by the water's edge, I let my spirit drift out into the ocean.

My spirit animal's eight arms reach out and I swim into them. She rocks me gently.

Holding on too long to Lah-ame's body is disrespectful to his spirit. A leader must help her people be strong, not drown in her own grief.

"Uido?" I hear Danna's voice and feel him giving my shoulder a little shake. "Come." He slips his arm around me and drags my unwilling body into the jungle. There he forces me to sit on a fallen log, pries my lips apart and dribbles water down my throat.

The cool water soothes me, like rain filling up the hollow of a dried-up stream.

Danna runs his strong fingers across my forehead, my cheeks, my chin. "Lah-ame will never truly leave us."

I return to the village with him. Seeing me, Mimi gathers the women and children together while Danna goes to tell the men I am ready. Kara and his hunters carry Lah-ame's body down from the platform. Kara pours the embers from the funeral fires into a torch and hands it to me. The elders remain behind to take the platform down and bury it beneath the tree.

"Where should we take Lah-ame?" Kara asks me.

"The cliff top," I say.

The women wail as we leave the village, myself at the head of the procession, taking the place of Lah-ame's family. Kara follows close behind, carrying Lah-ame single-handedly. Danna brings me Lah-ame's nautilus shell filled with water, then joins the other men who walk in a long line behind Kara.

My spirit animal's power surges into my arms, helping me to hold the torch aloft all the way toward the cliff. We reach the spot near the tall rock where Lah-ame used to pray. There I stop and plant the torch into the ground. Kara sets Lah-ame's body in the shadow of the rock and the men gather around in a circle.

I ease Lah-ame's chauga-ta off his neck and slide it over my head. His bone necklace drops softly into place beside my own, as though Lah-ame's ancestors know that I belong in their family now.

The men breathe on Lah-ame's face in a last farewell and return downhill one by one. Only Danna remains behind. The two of us take turns standing guard over Lah-ame's body the rest of that day and the following night. Together we tend to the torch so it does not go out.

At first light, I kneel and scratch at the ground with my bare hands to dig up enough earth to put the fire out. From my medicine pouch I take out a dried pitcher plant leaf and crush it between my fingers. The scent refreshes me. Holding my bone rattle above my head, I shake it. The rattle's sound fills my ears, together with the rush of the sea breeze, drowning out the loudest echoes of pain.

I will bury your grief beneath the ocean as you bury Lah-ame's body.

Danna and I work side by side, carving a deep hole into the earth with sharp rocks. I hear the mournful whistle of doves awaking in the jungle, *gu-roo, gu-roo.* But as the sun climbs higher, the *mita-tas'* whistles fade and we hear the cheerful *kan-wick, kan-wick* of terns diving for fish in the sea below. I feel that the birds' spirits are encouraging me to carry my people forward.

At last the hole is deep enough. I place the nautilus shell vessel inside and sit back on my haunches. "We bid you farewell, Lah-ame," I say.

We lower Lah-ame's body into the grave and pile earth back on top. The earth feels soft now, its touch comforting to my fingers. Our work done, I press my cheek against the mound of earth for a moment, wanting to get as close as possible to Lah-ame's remains. Then I stand up and Danna blows the dirt off my fingers. Facing east, I bow my head and scrub off the mourning clay that still sticks to my forehead.

In the bright sky spread out above us, I see an eagle soaring. It circles around us four times, so low that we can hear the beat of its wings. Then it glides away.

Together, we watch the eagle disappear into the sunshine.

"Down?" Danna asks.

Hand in hand, we walk back to join the rest of the tribe.

38

As soon as we are within sight of the village, Tawai runs up to us. "Uido, should we prepare for the feast now?" he asks.

I rest my hand on his thick curls as my people gather around me. "Lah-ame rests well," I say. "Tonight we will dance to celebrate his life."

Tawai pulls off the mourning palm leaves from the front of our hut and lays them in the center of the clearing. The other children follow his actions, shouting in happy anticipation of the feast ahead. Soon there is a huge pile of dry leaves, waiting for the evening's bonfire.

Natalang stands alone in front of her family's hut. I walk over to join her. "Would you like to go gathering together this morning?" I ask.

Her full lips part in a smile. "I was waiting for you, Uido," she says. I see Mimi nod with approval as we leave the clearing together, baskets in hand, Natalang's free arm tucked through mine.

"Uido, I have chosen the man I want to marry!" Natalang bursts out.

"Is it Ashu?" I try to sound enthusiastic.

"He gave me this!" She fingers a shell necklace that dangles between her breasts. Strung with bits of polished scallop shell, it glows pink, green and white, a rainbow of soft color. I am surprised that Ashu could make something so delicate.

"It is beautiful, Natalang," I tell her.

"Ashu is very attentive and loving," she says, describing my brother in a way I hardly recognize. "And yet he is so manly, too. He drew such intricate patterns on his legs during the scarification ceremony! It took him longer than anyone else. He had to use two tolma crystals to finish his tattoo, but he did not wince once." Looking at me sideways, she says, "Nor did Danna."

I say nothing.

"Danna's love could help you forget your grief over Lah-ame," Natalang suggests. She speaks for the rest of the day about how many babies she hopes to have after she marries Ashu, what she wants to name their babies, then about the other new couples in the tribe.

It feels good to listen to Natalang's cheerful voice again. But knowing how angry and jealous Ashu can be, I also worry a little, wishing Natalang had chosen a kinder man.

As daylight fades, we return to the village to help the women cook the evening meal. The men have brought back a great deal of food to honor Lah-ame's spirit: four monitor lizards, several boars, a large turtle, plenty of fish and crabs.

I enter Lah-ame's hut and bring out his fire tools.

Everyone seems to be watching me as I kneel down to start my first fire. But my nervousness disappears as I concentrate on the image of my spirit as a shining light kindling the wood. The muscles in my arms are so strong now that it feels easy to churn the fire stick in the hollow of the trunk with Lah-ame's vine rope. Soon I have a fire crackling.

Sitting in a circle around the fire, we each say a few words to thank Lah-ame's spirit for being among us. Then we eat until our bellies feel heavy. Once everyone has wiped their hands and picked their teeth clean, I carry Lah-ame's drum out into the clearing and beat out a dance rhythm. A circle of dancers forms, shoulders shaking, hips swaying, feet thumping.

I play until my palms are tired. Noticing the slowness of my hands, one of the elders finally takes over and frees me to dance out my feelings.

Joining the circle, I stamp and kick at my sadness until my feet feel light again, light enough to fly. Facing the fire, I lift my arms and whirl and soar the way an eagle does. I feel like a wind lifts me and blows power into my spirit. I weave in and out of the dancers, touching the bare shoulders of others with my eagle wings, the way Lah-ame touched all of our lives.

After I have danced myself to exhaustion, I leave the circle and sit in front of Lah-ame's hut. Natalang drops down next to me. Pearls of sweat glisten above her lips.

"I was glad to see you dancing, Uido," she says. "I know

you loved Lah-ame very much, but he would want you to be happy again, as soon as possible."

"It is hard," I say. "There is so much I wanted to ask him, so much we will never share now."

She nods and lays her soft hand on my arm. "So tell me about the strangers. Are they all as fat as Ragavan?"

I sense she is trying to cheer me up, but her words remind me of the hungry beggar child and the frail woman so broken in spirit. I shudder.

"If you will not tell me, I will have to find out myself," Natalang says.

"I am sorry, Natalang. It is difficult for me to speak of the strangers' world just now. Some of what I saw there was terrible. Thinking of it brings despair to my spirit."

"I really will see for myself soon," Natalang goes on. "I did not tell you yet, did I? Ashu and his friends are carving out a huge log to make the biggest canoe ever. The moment it is ready, we are going to visit the strangers' island!"

39

What?" I shout so loudly that some of the dancers turn to stare at me.

"I know you and Ashu fought about the strangers," Natalang says. "But surely now that they saved Tawai, you no longer dislike them."

"Natalang, listen to me—"

"Uido, I am tired of being on this little island all the time. So is Ashu."

"But their world has nothing that we need. You think they have a lot of food, but they do not share like we do. They let children of their tribe go hungry. You cannot imagine it."

She sighs. "I am sorry, Uido. I should have said nothing about the strangers."

"Natalang, I saw a woman there from another tribe like ours. She was thinner than anyone should ever be. Her spirit was lost in the strangers' world. Our spirits will die like hers if we try to live the way they do."

But Natalang is gazing at the dancers and my words do not seem to reach her. "Uido, let us not spoil the evening by fighting. I only wanted to cheer you up. I am truly sorry I upset you. Come, dance some more." She tugs at my hand.

I stand, but instead of joining the dancers again as she does, I look for Danna and pull him away from the circle.

"You look worried," he says.

I tell him what I heard from Natalang about Ashu's boat.

But Danna does not seem shocked at all. He pats my cheek and says, "The sea calls to many, Uido."

"Not you too?" For a moment I feel abandoned by how calm he acts.

"No, not me. This island is large enough to hold me as long as you stay here."

I open my mouth to speak again, but Danna's lips close over mine, forcing me to stop. He pulls my arms around his sturdy waist. We press together and I feel his heartbeat, strong and fast against my own chest.

"Uido," he whispers, "stop worrying about the tribe for now. First, you need to refresh your spirit with happy thoughts."

Danna is right. I feel too drained to fight with Ashu tonight. Or even to continue thinking about him and Natalang. My thoughts slow down as my hands wander across Danna's back, feeling the curve of his hips.

Danna's lips move to my earlobe. "I found a beautiful spot in the jungle a few days ago . . ."

I run my fingers over his mouth. "Shall we go there now?"

We wander out of the village into the soft blackness of

the jungle. In the distance, I hear the *uk-uk, coo-roo* of an owl.

Nestling together beneath the great black trunk of a moro-ta tree, we look at the moonlight dripping through its branches. Fireflies glow around us like fallen stars, and the scent of vanilla flowers drifts in the air.

For a while, nothing exists but the magic of shared silence and beauty of our togetherness.

40

Finally, Danna falls asleep, the ends of his mouth curving up in a gentle smile. I sit beside him for a few more moments, looking at his skin glisten in the moonlight as he sleeps. Then I get up and walk quietly back to my family's hut, thinking of the day Danna and I will have a hut of our own in the village. But in my dreams later that night, neither love nor beauty awaits me.

Instead, I see all the En-ge pouring onto the sea in great canoes, their bodies black and proud. They leave our island behind—the sky above it no longer pierced by our hunters' arrows, its jungles empty of our women's laughter. And far away on the strangers' island I hear Tawai's gleeful shrieks fade into frightened whimpers, while Natalang's plump body shrinks into that of a hunchbacked beggar.

The dream disturbs my sleep. Half awake, staring at the dark roof above me, I pray to the spirits, harder than I have ever prayed before.

"Biliku-waye," I beg, "please do something to help my people see that our ways can be stronger than the strangers' ways. Show me how to protect our faith and confidence, so that our spirits remain as bright as they are now."

My spirit drifts far into the Otherworld.

On the shore of our island, I see Biliku-waye. She is a woman again, a giant woman with eight arms.

"I heard your call for help," she says. "I will do what I can."

She swims into the ocean and dives beneath the waves. Deeper and deeper she goes until she is on the lightless sea floor. I sense her eight arms are grabbing hold of the sea floor, somewhere far away in the great depths.

"Monster waves will come at your island," she says. "Guide your people to safety and their confidence in you will never wane again. But doubt yourself and the last of the En-ge will be gone."

I wake up trembling like the ground I saw in my vision. But around me, my family sleeps on undisturbed. Kara snores at Mimi's side and her breathing rolls like a gentle breeze in our dark hut.

Wanting to make sure everything is peaceful as usual, I crawl out noiselessly. The village is a picture of calm. Moonlight flows over the empty clearing and the fire is a pile of gray ash. Everyone is asleep.

I circle around the huts but find nothing unusual. Resting my back against the trunk of the laurel tree behind Lah-ame's hut, I pull at the chauga-ta around my neck that once was his. "Lah-ame," I whisper, "what does my vision mean?" The bones of our ancestors seem to twitch under my fingers, but neither they nor Lah-ame can speak to me.

I rush to the beach, reaching it as the sun begins to rise.

"Sister, I need you!" I call out to my spirit animal.

In an instant, eight tentacles snake through the foam, reaching for me. I drift into the waves. Water presses in around me, red as blood in the dawn light.

Together, we swim down until we are at the bottom of the sea. There we stretch our arms out in eight directions until we sense an unusual swelling in the water, far to the south of my island. Over the uneven ocean floor we swim, tracking the swell to its source.

We reach a place where the sea floor is trembling. As we watch, the earth shudders and tears apart. One piece of it collapses, forming a pit, while another is thrust upward by the churning water, taking us with it.

Then I am standing on the beach again, in the bright sunshine of morning.

"What is happening?" I ask.

The stomach of the earth growls with hunger. This morning the sea will come at your island openmouthed, like a great shark, ready to swallow the village.

I shudder. "How can I save my people from it?"

Warn the tribe to take shelter. Tell them monster waves will rise out of the sea, threatening to drown your island. Lead them all to the cliffs.

"What if this is wrong?"

What if the ocean swallows the last of the En-ge because you did not warn them in time?

"Can you not give me another sign? Something I can show to prove my words are true?"

Move. Quickly.

"But the tribe may not believe me."

Go! Now!

"Wait," I call after my spirit animal as her body disappears beneath the shifting water. "Tawai already doubts our ways and maybe others do too. I cannot make a mistake now—not about such a terrible prediction."

But there is no answer.

41

I turn back and gaze in the direction of my village, nervously pulling at my chauga-ta. If I am wrong, surely my tribe will not give me another chance to be their oko-jumu.

I take a few hesitant steps up the beach. Running my hand over my medicine pouch, I think of my many journeys in the Otherworld and of my visions. I have never been wrong before.

As I leave the beach, I catch a difference in the sound of the waves—the faintest hint of a faraway hiss. When I enter the jungle, I drop down onto the soft mat of leaves and press an ear to the ground. Biliku-waye's laughter rumbles through it like buried thunder. I get up and lay my hand on the trunk of a coconut tree. I feel its spirit shaking like a mouse poisoned by a cobra's venom.

With my head bowed, I gather my courage and pray. "Biliku-waye, Pulug-ame, hold the ocean back until my tribe is safe."

I run straight back to the village, hoping to gather everyone together there. The jungle is unnaturally silent, except for the shrill *treee-tri-tri-tri* of a bee-eater bird. But this morning its call sounds like a warning rather than a song to greet the new day. Wet leaves cling to my feet as they thunder across the jungle floor. The breeze whistles past my ears, urging me on.

I storm into our village. A group of children playing in the clearing stops and stares at me, surprised to see me racing across without greeting anyone. The bachelor hut is nearly empty now and most of the men have already left to hunt. Of the girls, only a few late risers, including Natalang, remain. She turns her sleepy face in my direction, but I rush past her.

"Uido? Why are you in such a hurry?" one of the women calls out. She is echoed by others.

I make straight for Lah-ame's hut. My stomach cramps with pain from running so fast. Near the entrance I double over and stumble inside.

Mimi follows me into Lah-ame's hut. "Is something wrong, Uido?"

"We must go," I pant. "Now. To the cliff top."

"What?" Her tone sounds bewildered. "Why?"

Holding on to Mimi, I look for the waist-high drum that Lah-ame used to sound the alarm and gather the tribe together. But just as I lay my hands on it, we hear a shout coming from the beach. It is the voice of the ra-gumul boy who stands guard there.

"*Olaye, olaye, odo-lay, odo-lay!* Come, everyone! The strangers are here again!"

42

The boy's cries set a new panic swirling in my mind. If I beat out the alarm in the village now, some people might be confused about whether they should answer the boy's call and go to the beach or else follow the drumbeat and assemble in the clearing.

Perhaps I should gather everyone together at the beach instead of the village, to avoid any confusion. My eyes fall on the small drum with vine-rope straps that Lah-ame played the first time I went to the Otherworld. It is not as loud as his waist-high drum, but it is easier to carry.

With Mimi's help, I slip the vine ropes tied to the drum over my shoulders. Straightening my back and flattening my palms, I beat on the drum and stride into the clearing. *Come, En-ge, come.*

As I sound the call, the giant squid's power floods my body. It feels as though I have grown eight arms. I slap harder and faster at the drum's mouth. *Come, En-ge, come.*

The elders gape at me. But they are the first to stop their work and group together behind me. The women follow, strapping their babies to their backs or holding little children by the hand. I look over the crowd for Tawai, but he is not among them. I fear he has run away to meet the strangers already.

Still pounding on the drum, I motion for my people to come with me, out of the village and onto the beach. As we walk, my urgent call echoes through the jungle and across the wide sands.

Close to the water, at the south end of the beach, I see a small group of people. Ragavan and his two men have landed there as usual. They toss colorful buckets out of their boat and onto the sand. While I beat the drum, more En-ge emerge from the jungle. Ashu and his friends arrive, but they ignore my call and race past the growing crowd to join Ragavan.

Halfway down the beach, I stop. Danna bursts through the trees, elbows his way past the others and stands at my side. "I was searching for you. What is wrong?"

I squeeze his hand gently. "I had a frightening vision last night and had to call on my spirit animal. Something terrible is about to happen." I explain it to him quickly and then count the tightly knotted family groups. Once I am certain the entire tribe is on the beach, I finally let my hands rest on the drum. Danna stands close at my side.

I hear Tawai shriek with delight. He has climbed into Ragavan's boat to help the strangers unload. "Look!" He throws different-colored buckets into the air one after another. "I am making a rainbow!"

Distracted by his antics, a few children strain to break

away from their families. Even some of the adults look with interest at the strangers' gifts. But then Kara pushes through the crowd and steps toward the strangers' boat.

Seeing him approach, Ragavan and his men crouch down on the sand. Kara's presence sends Tawai, Ashu, and his friends reluctantly back to the edge of our group.

At last, all eyes turn to me.

"Listen, my people. Last night I had a vision. A giant wave will roll out of the ocean and drown us all unless we move to higher ground at once."

My words seem to confuse the crowd. Many young men shake their heads in disbelief, while the girls whisper to one another.

"What do you mean, Uido?" a woman asks.

One of Kara's hunters says loudly, "How could she know such a thing?"

"Last night I had a terrible vision," I say. "My spirit animal took me beneath the ocean to help me understand this vision. There, I saw the earth shake and heard the ocean growling with hunger. Giant waves will rise up from the sea and roll across our island this morning. We must climb to safety or we will drown."

"But why?" An elder's voice carries across the confused babble. "Did someone upset Pulug-ame?"

"Perhaps Pulug-ame is angry because a woman wants to be our oko-jumu," Ashu suggests. His friends laugh.

Mimi glares at Ashu. "If one of my children angered the spirits, it was you," she says. "You lit a fire using the strangers' fire twigs. My daughter has never done anything wrong."

I raise my hand for silence. "Our beach will be underwater very soon. We *must* leave for the cliffs at once!"

But Ashu shouts, "Uido is weak. She did not save Tawai, the strangers did. Has everyone forgotten how my sister ran to their shores begging for help?" I see many ragumul boys nodding in agreement. Encouraged by their response, Ashu continues, "Uido is a coward." He points at Ragavan and his men. "The strangers' magic is stronger than hers. Tawai has told us of it, and I have shown you how well their fire twigs work. If the sea was going to swallow this island today, do you think the strangers would be here now?"

My people's eyes dart in confusion from my brother's smoldering face to mine.

"Ragavan," Ashu says, "show us the gifts you brought."

Ragavan seems to understand what Ashu wants him to do. He clambers into his canoe and pulls out a long stretch of red cloth. He waves it at us and the cloth flaps in the breeze, flowing out behind him like a stream of blood.

"We can all have beautiful things if we go to the strangers' world. Powerful magic too." Ashu's voice blazes with anger. "Follow me there!"

"You have no right to speak this way," Kara roars. I am pleased to hear many people murmur in support of his words. But I do not want to see my brother fight our father.

I hold up my hand again for silence. "Ragavan and his people have nothing that we need. On their island I saw a woman from a tribe like ours whose spirit had been killed by the strangers' cruel ways. She did not even have enough to eat—she had to beg for food. If we leave our island, the strangers will take away our land to cut down our trees—"

"Cut down our trees?" Ashu interrupts. "Why? Tawai said the things they have are better than ours. Their magic and their medicines are stronger, too. They cured Tawai."

"I do not deny their magic is powerful," I say. "But so is ours."

"If our medicines work so well, Uido, why did you row Tawai across to them?" Ashu crosses his arms with a smirk.

"Yes, Uido, answer that!" one of Ashu's friends shouts.

"Tawai's fascination with the strangers weakened his spirit," I explain. "He caught an illness they carried, a lau that made his spirit roam out of his body. I crossed the waters to retrieve his spirit. Without it, the strangers would never have been able to save him. So it was not only the strangers who healed him—I did too, by bringing his body and spirit together."

To my surprise, Tawai's shrill voice carries across the crowd. "That is true! My sister helped the strangers heal me."

At his words, the tribe becomes still. I feel for an instant as if the waves have stopped moving.

"What do you mean?" Ashu shouts.

"The strangers needed Uido's help," Tawai replies. "Maya, their oko-jumu, told me so. She said the strangers could not save me on their own. I think my spirit entered my body only because Uido called to it."

For an instant, my heart leaps with delight. The old Tawai who admired me seems to have returned. I watch the tribe listening intently to him and sense his sudden support is helping to convince them to follow me. But I have no time to thank my brother for this unexpected gift.

"I admit that I do not know everything that will happen," I say. "Sometimes when my spirit has a vision of the future, it is like peering through the thickness of the jungle at night. But other times I can see more clearly than if I stood on the cliff top and saw with the eyes of an eagle. So, my people, I tell you now: the killing wave will come and we must flee."

As I finish, a sea eagle streaks down from the cliff toward the beach. The great bird's shadow falls over us. It circles low over my head four times, its wings thrashing. There is warning in every line of its movement.

Voices cry out from the crowd: "A sign!" "The sea eagle!" "Did you see how suddenly it appeared?"

A shudder runs through the earth. The coconut trees on the beach sway as though a sudden gust of wind blows through them. A few of the children whimper like frightened animals and a little baby screeches in terror. Even Kara's hunters look concerned.

Just then Tawai bursts out, "The tide is moving very far out! Look!"

I glance at the ocean. The tide has dropped much lower than usual. Stranded fish hop on the sand that was underwater moments ago. And the waters are retreating still farther.

"Uido, the sea is shrinking," Natalang cries. "It is the opposite of what you said would happen."

"Clearly, Uido is wrong." Ashu laughs. "And unlike my sister, I am not frightened by every tremble in the ground. If you are brave, come with me."

"The waves will return to tear us apart," I say to my people. "We are losing precious moments. We must go. Now."

Ashu folds his arms across his chest, his legs spread apart. "Stay here and prove your courage," he challenges. "Men should not run like frightened rats."

"Ashu, this is not something to play at." Feeling frantic, I rush to him and clasp his wrists. "You are risking all our lives. Listen to me for once."

He shakes me off.

"Natalang," I plead, hoping that she can help Ashu see reason, "tell him to come with us."

"You would choose my sister over me?" Ashu asks her.

"Natalang, please." I pull at her soft hands.

She stares into my eyes, her own eyes wide with fear. But she steps away from me and takes my brother's hand. "I should stay." Her voice shakes.

Behind us, I hear Tawai squealing, "Let me get some fish! I will follow later." I turn to find him struggling to break Kara's grip on his arm.

I feel sure that to leave anyone behind would be to leave them to a certain death and I desperately want to convince

Ashu. But there is no more time. Any moment now the sea will rush back and drown us all.

Already I have risked the safety of my people by wasting precious moments with my brother.

I do not want to split the tribe as Lah-ame did long ago. But I see no other choice.

Raising my arms to the skies, I call out, "Biliku-waye, Pulug-ame, protect us." To my tribe I cry, "Follow me, En-ge! To the cliffs!"

43

With Danna at my side, I move toward the cliffs as fast as I can without breaking into a panicked run. I hear footsteps behind us, like the first drops of rain before a storm. The sound grows, quickly becoming as loud as a thunderstorm.

Only when I sense that most of the tribe is with me do I allow myself a backward glance. To my relief, Kara and Mimi are dragging Tawai between them. I see Danna's brothers, his grandfather, Mimi's sister and her family, other aunts, uncles and cousins of mine. Many of the ragumul are at the tail end of the crowd, still looking unsure whether they should be following me or Ashu. A few of the women keep looking back as well, as though they have left someone behind.

I cannot see Natalang or Ashu anywhere.

"Keep going," I tell my people, fighting to keep panic out of my voice.

We enter the jungle at the foot of the cliff and trample over the undergrowth. The ground shudders again. Seeing the trees shake, I fear they might fall and crush us to death. For a moment, I even worry that once we get to the cliff, it may be torn off and hurled into the ocean.

But it is too late to doubt myself. "Faster!" I shout, staying at the head of the group and quickening my pace.

As I lead my people upward, I see a viper slither past my toes, climbing the rise as fast as it can. Four rats follow it, squeaking loudly, but in its hurry the snake ignores the easy meal.

"Look!" one of the elders shouts from close behind me. "The animals know Uido is right. Their spirits have sensed danger, too."

Encouraged by those words, I leap across the stream gushing down from the cliff. At my feet, a water snake wriggles upward like a band of earth come alive. At the same time, a monitor lizard, nearly as long as Tawai is tall, waddles along our path. The jungle is emptying out—animals that usually sleep during the day, animals that usually eat one another, all making for higher ground.

As the slope grows steeper and the trees give way to bushes, I see more animals huddled together close to the tree line. My heart thuds painfully against my ribs, but I keep moving, up, up, up.

Stones cut at my feet as we move across the rocky stretch. Yet we keep climbing higher, until at last we reach the flat top of the cliff.

Far below us, the sea's voice has dulled into a distant murmur. Standing near Lah-ame's grave, in the shadow of his prayer rock, I stop and turn to face my people.

I can smell fear in the sweat pouring off our bodies.

Couples lean on one another wearily, while children cling to their mothers' legs. Many of the elders collapse on the ground, exhausted. Even a few of the ra-gumul boys wobble as they try to remain standing.

"Group into families, so I can tell who is missing," I call out.

As my people obey, I see that Kara's arms are curled around Mimi's sobbing body. His jaw is tightly clenched, as though he is trying to hold back his tears over Ashu. Tawai hangs on to Mimi's grass skirt, his eyes wide with confusion. I hear Natalang's mother wailing as her family bunches together.

When I finish counting, I realize that four of our ra-gumul are not with us: Ashu has stayed behind with his two best friends, and Natalang remains on the beach with them too. I long to rush back through the jungle and bring them to safety, but I know it is too late. Instead I scramble up to the top of Lah-ame's rock to see as much as I can, while the rest of my tribe remains on the cliff top just below me.

The beach looks almost unrecognizable now. The tide has gone so far out that the curved stretch of white sand is twice as wide as usual. Sea creatures are writhing everywhere, like nightcrawler worms blinded by daylight.

I see Natalang, Ashu and his two friends running between branches of coral, scooping up armloads of fish. Further out, Ragavan and his men are grouped around their boat, which has been stranded on a sand bank by the retreating tide.

Then the ocean's rumble loudens into a warning hiss. The tide changes direction in the distance.

I watch with horror as the sea charges back with a fury I have never seen before. Giant waves swell like cobras spreading their hoods to kill. Spray flies like venom dripping from curved fangs.

The water rolls over Ragavan's boat. I hear the crunch of splintering wood, the clang of metal against metal, the wails of pain cut suddenly off. In an instant, the men are gone—there is only water where they were standing, water that is growing taller as it rages closer to land.

Ahead of the tide, four black streaks race inward. Natalang, Ashu and his friends are running for their lives and all I can do is pray for their safety.

"Ashu! My son!" Mimi's terrified voice reaches my ears.

I see the earth quaking in front of my brother and his friends, while behind them the sea keeps gaining ground. One of the figures stumbles.

I tear my gaze away from them and shut my eyes. But the noise of the oncoming water is even more terrifying. I hear the grinding of stone against stone as blocks of coral are tossed around like tiny pebbles. It sounds as though the spirits have lost control of their power and forgotten everything they created.

My eyes open again to see the first line of waves striking land halfway up our beach, with a crash so loud it seems to split my head apart. The coconut tree that Tawai fell from topples into the water. The first waves try to return oceanward, but they are dragged back toward land by the next group of waves. Stronger and fiercer than the first, the second line looks ready to swallow the island whole. It climbs over the receding water, gaining height, then tumbles down at the edge of the jungle in a confusion of blue and white. As it tries to roll back into the sea, the third swell approaches. Waves smash into waves traveling in the opposite direction, making spray leap into the air like rain going the wrong way. And all the water is pushed landward again.

With each passing instant, the sea is piling up on itself and we can do nothing but watch. Our beach is now completely underwater. Our canoes are hurled backward.

I see Kara shudder, while Mimi holds on to Tawai. His hands are shaking as he hides his face. Women clutch children to their breasts. Even some of our strongest hunters are cowering. Danna's body alone remains still as a rock.

The ocean continues its fight to drown more land. Monster waves push against the jungle, pelting the trees with blocks of coral. A huge beech tree totters, and I hear a tremendous splash as it falls in and swirls in the water like a capsized boat.

As far as I can see, the outer ring of our island lies beneath the seething ocean. Still, the waves rage on. I pray they will not destroy our village.

The ocean snakes through the jungle, biting at the great trunks of ancient trees. Some fall, but many stand firm. They block the sea's path, weakening it; but not before the clearing where our village stood is completely filled with water. Not one hut could possibly remain standing.

Then at last the waves slither back again.

A second tremor shakes the island. But this time only the sand is drowned, and the jungle is not disturbed by the rush of water.

The rest of the morning is full of noises and movement. A few more times the sea rises and falls back. But each group of waves is smaller and weaker, until soon after midday the sea coils lazily around our island again like a python with its belly full. I sense that the ocean's spirit is tired at last and that it will not come at us again.

I climb down from the rock, my eyes aching from staring for so long at the sunshine bouncing off the water. My people press in around me to ask if I can sense who among those on the beach is still alive. But rather than trying to search for the answer, I tell them to rest.

Kara says, "Shall I tell my hunters to gather food for the tribe, Uido?"

"Perhaps we should give the animals' spirits time to rest as well," I suggest.

He nods. "I will tell them to bring no meat back yet."

After he sends the hunters into the jungle, I lead Kara, Natalang's father and the two fathers of the missing ragumul down to the beach. I notice that the water flowing from the cliff is still clear and fresh, at least in the upper reaches. But as we move lower, it becomes muddy and undrinkable.

The closer we get to the beach, the harder our walk

becomes. We clamber over many uprooted trunks and fallen tree limbs. In some places, broken branches dangle overhead, threatening to crash down any moment. And the shaking earth has carved out pits that have filled up with seawater.

"The air will be thick with mosquitoes soon," one of the men mutters, staring at the muddy pools dotting the jungle floor.

When we step onto the beach, what I see is more frightening than even the swamp. The breeze stinks of drying seaweed, dead fish, and flesh that is already starting to rot in the heat. Rocks, broken coral, bits of wood, twisted pieces of metal torn off Ragavan's boat, and the brightly colored buckets that were his last gifts to us lie scattered on the once-white sand.

Corpses must lie there too.

I turn my gaze away from land to the sea. The shallows are no longer clear and blue-green but muddy. Ugly specks of black and brown whirl on the foam. Pieces of the reef have been thrust up out of the water and they claw at the sky.

"Let us look for people," I say to the men, who are also staring in horror at the misshapen beach. We pick our way across. One of the men points to a human leg sticking out of the sand. Together, he and Kara dig up the body of one of the strangers.

From farther down the beach, Natalang's father shouts, "Another stranger is here."

It is a torn body—all that remains of Ragavan. His body

is broken in two and his intestines are hanging out. The sight makes me want to vomit, but I force myself to help carry his corpse. We lay it down near the jungle's edge, well out of reach of the waves.

Staring at Ragavan, I feel relief and sadness mix inside me like mud and water. Despite all the problems he caused, my mind still has clear images of Ragavan helping clean Tawai's wound on this beach and handing my little brother a box of fire twigs. As much as Maya is my friend, Tawai and Ragavan were friends. Maybe he has a son who is Tawai's age who will grieve for him. There is so much I never knew about Ragavan and will never find out.

We continue searching the beach for human remains. Of the third stranger, we find no more than a bloated arm floating in one of the pools. One of the men finds a crushed foot and another a piece of thigh. The parts are so misshapen that we cannot tell if both were torn off the same body—or even whether they belonged to one of our people rather than another of the strangers.

After a thorough search, we find nothing else and I decide we must stop.

Kara points at the remains. "What shall we do?"

"We will bury them all in the jungle, as we bury our own people," I reply. "Perhaps these men meant well, perhaps not. But others like them will come again. And we must treat the strangers with respect if the strangers are ever to respect us in return."

Silently, we drag them into the jungle. We dig a great hole and cover them all with earth.

The sun is setting when we climb back uphill toward the cliffs. In the fading light, my spirit feels heavy with guilt about the deaths I did not prevent.

"I never even tried to warn the strangers about the wave," I say to Kara. "I thought only of the tribe's safety."

"But you saved us all, Uido," Kara says softly.

"Perhaps not even that," I reply, thinking of the misshapen thigh and the crushed foot.

44

We reach the others on the cliff at dusk. Kara's hunters have brought back fruit and berries and roots and nuts that we all share for our evening meal. Everyone has questions but I sit apart from the rest of the tribe, unwilling to answer them, though I know I must talk to them soon.

After we have eaten, I rise to explain that we must remain on the cliff until the jungle is safe enough for us to return. But just as I begin, a woman shouts, "Look! Look! They are back!"

Through the darkness I see three figures stumbling up the slope. With shouts of surprise and welcome, my people run to greet them. Ashu is limping along, his arms around his friends' shoulders, his left leg swollen to four times its usual size. He winces with every step, but his two friends seem to have outrun the waves without getting badly hurt. They set him down and crouch together at my feet.

"Where is Natalang?" I ask, clinging to a desperate hope that she might not be gone.

"Dead." The word bursts out of Ashu like a sob. I hear

some people moan. But all I can think is that I will never again hear the sound of Natalang's laughter bubbling out of her like foam on the sea.

"How did it happen?" Natalang's mother wails.

"She—" Ashu's voice breaks. "We were gathering fish together. I heard the noise of the water rushing back. We looked up and saw a blue-green wall of water coming at us. Natalang was too frightened to move. I tried to drag her away and she started running, holding tightly to my hand. But then the ground cracked into pieces in front of us. She slipped and fell and I lost her." Ashu pulls at his hair.

"Did you see her drown?" I sense the impossible want in Natalang's mimi's voice. "Maybe my daughter is still alive."

"No." Ashu's voice cracks. "I saw her body twisted out of shape, bleeding where her leg used to be. It was drifting far away in the water, out of reach."

Ashu seems to crumple into himself. His friends do not dare look up at me.

The crowd around us falls quiet. I feel everyone's eyes on me, waiting to see what I will do. Staring out at the blue ocean where Natalang's body now lies, I feel a dull anger growl inside me like a faraway storm. For a moment, I wish Ashu were dead.

Do you truly want that?

I look down at Ashu. His lips are gray as ash, his bruised skin dark as burned wood. But though his body is hurt, I sense that his spirit's pain is far greater.

Ashu loved Natalang. And no matter what I could have done, Natalang would have stayed with him because she loved him.

Spirits may punish and destroy. An oko-jumu should not. Your arms are strong. Strong enough to throw away your anger.

My friend is gone, without a proper burial. The only way I can honor Natalang's spirit is to forgive the man she loved.

My people have formed a great ring around me. I sense they are waiting for me to act, to teach, to guide.

A breeze cools my forehead.

Your hands are those of a healer. Hold your brother in them. It is what Natalang would want.

"You are welcome back," I say slowly. Then I tend to my brother and his friends. Kneeling next to Ashu, I untie my medicine bundle. I tell all three boys to lie down. Into their foreheads, I rub drops of the insect-eating plants' healing juice to lighten their spirits.

Next, I attend to their bodies. When I am done applying medicines, I ask the men to bring me wood and several lengths of vine. Using pieces of wood, we make crutches and a splint for Ashu. With Kara's help, I straighten Ashu's broken bone, then set and bind it using the vine rope.

After I am done, I make way for everyone else to greet the survivors. Most of the tribe presses close around them, weeping and laughing. It is a strange reunion, joy mixing with sorrow like waves from different directions crashing into one another. Only Natalang's family sits apart.

Ashu's fingers twist through his hair and his body jerks with sobs.

"Uido," he says. "I need to go to Natalang's family." With my help, he limps over to them. Bending down awkwardly before her parents, he says, "I am sorry."

Natalang's mimi looks up at us. Her eyelids are swollen and her face is wet. But she opens her arms and pulls me onto her lap. "You were her friends," she says, her voice small and tired. "She loved you both."

We stay with her as the gloom of dusk deepens into the black depths of night. Then she lets us go and rocks back and forth in her husband's arms.

The tribe mourns Natalang's death long into the night.

As the moon begins to travel down the sky again, I go from person to person and embrace each of them. And imagining myself inside my spirit animal's eight-armed body, I pull some of the grief and shock out of their spirits and into my own. One by one, my people fall asleep on the bare ground.

Then I let my tired body sink into Danna's arms, but my spirit swims restlessly in and out of sleep. My mind is heavy with sadness and guilt. The five deaths weigh it down like great rocks—Natalang's most of all.

While moonlight still shines over the watery edges of our island, I leave Danna's side and crawl up the tall rock, slow as a snail. Reaching the top, I call out to my spirit animal.

Together, we dive into the protection of an underwater

cave. There the weight of my grief feels lighter and she helps me push it slowly away.

Natalang is not truly gone. Death cannot separate the spirits of friends. She will meet you again, in visions of the Otherworld.

At dawn, my spirit animal forces me out of the cave and gently up through the water. When we reach the surface, I pour out more of my grief and watch it flow like blood into the ocean. Then I land on the rock again. But now my back is as straight as a spear, strong enough to carry what remains of our sadness.

45

I reach Danna's side just as he is waking up.

"Look," he says to me, pointing up at the sky.

In the distance, I see a black dot that, like Ragavan's boat, is growing so fast that it must be from the strangers' world. As the dot comes closer to our island, a terrible noise shakes the sky.

"A flying boat!" one of the elders shouts, but it is not the fish-shaped kind we have seen before. This one is fat and its wings whir in a circle above it.

It drops lower and lower, hovering closer to us than any flying boat has ever dared, making a loud *ka-tek-tek-tek* noise as though it is chopping the sky. I see some hunters grab their bows and aim their arrows at it, while children cower on the ground.

But the strangers' magic no longer scares me, because I know it is not more powerful than ours—just different. Looking up at the flying boat, I recognize the familiar shape of a woman sitting inside.

"They are friends," I say, once it has passed and I can make myself heard. We watch the flying boat land on a bare patch of ground farther away on the cliff. Maya jumps out and runs across the rocky earth toward us.

Tawai shouts, "This is the woman who healed me."

"Uido." Maya flings her arms around me. "I am afraid all En-ge die."

Hearing her speak our language, my people murmur with amazement.

"We survived," I tell Maya. "All but one of us."

"Uido warned us to flee," Danna says. "She knew the ocean would try to eat the island."

"But—" Maya breaks off.

"You knew, surely?" Tawai says.

"How, Uido?" Maya's face shows her confusion. "How you can know such thing?"

"You must have known," Tawai says. "Your world is full of magic."

My tribe presses in closer, eager to hear Maya's reply.

"No." She shakes her head. "We do not know wave is coming." For a few moments, she chokes up. "Many people in my tribe die. More than all En-ge. Many, many hundreds."

I hear cries of shock from the crowd. "Uncle Paleva?" I ask.

Her lip trembles, but she bites it and then says, "He is hurt. Badly. Soon, he dies. I do not want to come here. I want to stay with my uncle. But he says I must go. Find En-ge. Help you."

Maya covers her face with her hands, as though tears are something to be ashamed of. I put my arm around her, but she does not sob. Wiping her tears away with the back of her hand, she asks, "How we can help you?" She points to the flying boat. "We bring food and medicines. What we can do?"

"We do not need your help," I say gently. "It is enough that you have come to offer it. Go back and tell your uncle we are well, so that his spirit will enter the Otherworld happy."

Maya gazes down at the jungle, where fallen trees lie like scattered twigs, and at the beach, where coral has washed up like broken bones. "Your village is gone?"

"It does not matter. We will rebuild it together. I will look after my people from now on."

"Uido, I am not Ragavan. I want to help your tribe."

"Ragavan is dead," Tawai interrupts.

"Dead?" Maya stares at me.

"Yes," I reply. "They came to visit us and the wave killed him and his two men. We treated their bodies with respect. They are buried in our jungle."

"How could Ragavan not know the wave was coming?" Tawai asks.

"Our magic does not always work," Maya says. "Our medicines do not always work. Much we do not know. We do not see waves come and many die."

I turn to my people. In their eyes, I see the same respect they once gave Lah-ame. I even hear many of the ra-gumul boys murmuring words of support. And my spirit senses the tribe's deepening faith and love.

"I know we can trust you," I say to Maya. "But the

En-ge must be alone now. If we need your help again, we will find you. I came to your island once, for my brother's sake. And I may do so again someday."

Maya looks unhappy. "I wish we can help somehow. Please. I do not understand why you say no."

"Uncle Paleva would," I say to her. "But there is one thing you can do, Maya."

"Tell me it." Her face brightens a little. "I do what you want."

"Help continue Uncle Paleva's work. Help keep strangers away from us."

She puts her hand on her chest. "Yes, Uido. I do that."

"And if his spirit waits until you return, tell Uncle Paleva I wish him a good crossing into the Otherworld. Lah-ame's spirit journeyed there only a few days ago. He is surely waiting to greet his old friend again."

"I am sorry Lah-ame is gone," Maya says softly. "No other thing I can do?"

"Perhaps, with your help, your people and mine may share these islands and learn from each other. Thank you for caring about us, Maya. May your heart be in a good place."

She repeats my words of farewell. "*Ngig kuk-l-ar-beringa*, Uido."

Tawai leaps up into Maya's arms. When he lets her go, she walks back to her flying boat. Before she gets in, she turns to me and waves her hand back and forth.

I raise my own hand to mimic her gesture of farewell.

She forces her lips into a smile and climbs into the flying boat. The black wings on top whirr faster than a hummingbird's, then disappear as it rises straight into the air. I wave until the flying boat shrivels into a black spot and is lost from view.

46

For the rest of the day, my people keep busy with work. Kara and his hunters fetch coconuts from the beach. Other men set about making tools and vessels. While the women go gathering in the upper reaches of the jungle, Danna helps me carve a new set of fire tools. We speak of the work that lies ahead—the rebuilding of our village, how long we must wait before we fish again, what animals we can soon hunt.

At dusk, fireflies glow around us. The sea has forgotten its anger. We listen to the gentle waves slosh back and forth as we gather to share the evening meal. The wind changes direction and it no longer carries the smell of death up to us from beach. Instead, it brings a new scent from far across the water. I kindle a warm blaze and Kara feeds the fire with dried coconut leaves. Then we stand together in a circle and I lead the chant to honor the spirits for their gifts of fire and food.

I watch the flames leap like red-orange snakes, twisting together and then slithering apart. The fire keeps changing shape from one instant to the next, yet somehow it also remains the same. So, too, in the face of whatever awaits us, I shall ensure that my people's spirits never weaken, that we never lose our true selves.

The firelight throws brightness and darkness on the faces of my people. In their eyes, I see strands of hope. These I will braid together into a strong rope to pull ourselves into the future. But first I must wash away the last of our sadness and help those around me who have suffered great loss. As Lah-ame would have done.

Standing against the blaze, I say a prayer of my own making to my people.

"Biliku-waye, Pulug-ame, and all the spirits of the Otherworld, protect us, the En-ge people, and keep us forever safe.

"For a long time we filled the islands with love, and we filled one another with love. Our songs drifted across the seas but we did not care what lay elsewhere, for we had it all, everything we needed, here.

"But that time is gone. The strangers will return when storms do not keep them away from us. And other En-ge will cross over, just as I did.

"Yet our life on these islands is far from over.

"If, on some days, it seems that the strangers' ways are more powerful than our own, let us climb up here, watch the sea tickle the feet of the cliff, and remember this:

"With our ancient wisdom, we escaped the great wave that killed hundreds of strangers. The spirits told us of the coming of the killing wave; the wave the strangers did not see despite all their magic. Those who believed in the En-ge ways, we who kept our faith, were spared the largeness of grief that struck their world.

"And so I tell you, my people, as we prepare for whatever the future holds: the new journey awaiting us is not death. It is another life."

My people's eyes grow as bright as the crackling fire that fills the air with warmth.

Ashu stands up, wobbling slightly, but his voice is steady as he says, "Thank you for my life, Uido-waye."

Has my brother really said *waye* after my name?

As though in answer to my silent question, Kara rises, his chest swelling with a joyous breath. "Another life, Uido-waye!" he shouts.

Mimi throws her long arms up toward the sky. My tribe takes up the chant. "Another life, Uido-waye!"

The chant grows faster, stronger. It spills over the cliff and rolls across the ocean. It echoes through the jungle and leaps from the uneven land below to the unbroken world above. I run the tips of my fingers over the chauga-ta around my neck, wondering if the voices are loud enough to reach Lah-ame's spirit. In the warm breeze that strokes my cheeks, I feel the caress of his breath. I see a faint glow stretching across the ocean, as though the spirits of our ancestors and all the oko-jumu who came before me are smiling at us.

But then Danna's arm slides around my waist. He pulls me back into the bright circle of the living. "Uido-waye, shall we dance?" he asks. "Or are you still worrying about something?"

"I am not worried at all," I reply.

"Then come, oko-jumu. Quickly, before our problems weigh you down again. Let us not waste precious moments when your spirit dances like moonlight on water." Danna's shoulders shake with laughter.

I begin to laugh, too, with all of my body. My laughter reaches into the pit of my stomach and the ends of my toes. In triumph, I raise my hands to the sky, then I slap my thighs with my palms. My bones feel as strong as the great reefs of coral, and my mind as clear as the water of a rushing stream.

Suddenly, all of us are swaying together, laughing at the top of the cliff. And Danna's feet match mine as we beat out a rhythm of celebration, in perfect unison, on the warm earth of our island.

AUTHOR'S NOTE

It seems unbelievable that in today's world there are human beings who live the way they did thousands of years ago, who refuse to make contact with modern civilization. A few native tribes living in the Andaman Islands of India still struggle to preserve their culture by keeping to themselves in the face of increasing encroachment by modern settlers from the Indian mainland. Though these tribes may go back seventy thousand years, their populations are shockingly low. Recent estimates of the combined count for living members of the Jarawa, Great Andamanese, Onge, Sentinelese and Shom Pen tribes ranged from four hundred to a thousand at the time I started writing this book, some years ago. But the Great Andamanese are thought to have become extinct since then. The future of these ancient people is in jeopardy and they face several grave threats to their survival—including the destruction of their habitat and cultural traditions.

In 1994, on a research trip to the Andaman Islands, I stayed for a brief while in the jungle where the last remaining Onge live. Thus, I am fortunate to count myself among the very few people in this world who have had at least passing contact with an ancient mode of life that pulses with its own special beauty.

When the tsunami of December 26, 2004, wreaked

destruction across the globe, several "primitive" groups living on the Andaman Islands escaped to safety. Amazingly, they somehow avoided the killer wave that caused a shockingly high death toll in our modern times. In January 2005, an Associated Press reporter met four tribesmen named Ashu, Tawai, Danna and Lah, who said that their entire tribe (over two hundred strong) had survived. An ancient knowledge of the movement of wind and oceans and a sensitivity to the behavior of sea birds and island creatures may have warned these native people to flee inland in the nick of time. We do not know precisely how they realized that disaster was about to strike or why they were able to take appropriate action. Here, I have used my imagination, in conjunction with research, observation of the tribes and my experience with them, to tell a plausible story of what might have helped one such tribe remain relatively unscathed by this terrible natural disaster.

The opening incident in the book is also based on reports of an actual standoff between the Sentinelese tribe and the crew of a Portugese freighter that was shipwrecked off North Sentinel Island in the 1980s.

My training is in the physics and chemistry of the oceans, not anthropology. In writing this book, I spoke to anthropologists and researched texts and peer-reviewed literature to augment my understanding of indigenous people who once lived or still survive on the Andaman and Nicobar islands. The language, customs and beliefs expressed stem from ethnographic studies of native

Andaman Islanders. However, I chose to give Uido's tribe a fictional name (*En-ge* simply means "people" in the language of the tribe I met on the islands). This helped free me to amalgamate my knowledge and experience to fit Uido's story—and to remember that I was writing neither an anthropological nor oceanographic text but a novel. Inspired by the spirit of Jorge Luis Borges, I gave my first loyalty in the telling of this tale "to the dream": Uido's dream.